THIRTEEN GRAVES

ORION GRACE

OG

First Edition
Copyright © 2025 by Orion Grace
All rights reserved. No part of this publication may be reproduced, stored in a retrieval system, or transmitted in any form or by any means—electronic, mechanical, photocopying, recording, or otherwise—without the prior written permission of the author, except for brief quotations used in reviews or scholarly works.
This is a work of fiction. Names, characters, places, and incidents are either the product of the author's imagination or used fictitiously. Any resemblance to actual persons, living or dead, events, or locales is entirely coincidental.

ISBN: 9798282916010

Cover design by Lance Buckley Design

Printed and published in the United Kingdom.
For more information,
visit: www.oriongracebooks.com

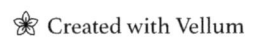

❀ Created with Vellum

To my wife, my first reader, my hobbit from the real Shire

THE MORRISON FAMILY TREE

Norah Morrison, *matriarch and grand-mother.*

ELLIS MORRISON, *Norah's eldest son, married to* **Violette**.
 * **Leon Morrison**, *their son, married to* **Melissa**.
 * **Charlie Morrison**, *their daughter, married to* **Kacey**.

ALICIA POWELL (NÉE MORRISON), *Norah's daughter, married to* **Julian**.

PATRICK MORRISON, *Norah's youngest son, married to* **Lottie**.
 * **Tilly Morrison**, *their 16-year-old daughter.*
 * ***Timothy Morrison***, *deceased at 4 years old, 19 years ago.*

KILLIAN MORRISON, *Norah's nephew.*
 * **Rebecca Morrison**, *his daughter, in a relationship with* **Tristan**.

* **Flynn Morrison,** *his son.*

1

TRISTAN

Rebecca assured me long driveways are very common in the countryside, though she admitted not *this* long. The private driveway leading to her ancestral home is thirty-eight miles long. To put this in perspective, that is roughly the diameter of the M25 ring road around London, or three times the length of Manhattan Island. Or a farm track in the Scottish Highlands, I guess.

It took just under an hour in a car from the moment we entered their estate until we could see the house. I mean, think of the cost of just filling in the potholes. By the time you've fixed all of them, new ones have popped up. And does the postman drive all the way down to deliver the Advertiser Monthly brochure, or do the residents have to drive an hour to pick it up from a post box at the top of the track? It took us two days to get here from London to make the six hundred-mile drive more bearable, but this last hour was by far the longest – and the most fascinating.

The Morrison estate spans ten thousand acres of pure wilderness. All the lochs (yes, plural) we drove past, the glen, the herds of cattle, the wide open spaces, all part of the same estate. The entire way down the private track, I couldn't help but wonder if I was going to spend a week with the laird and lady of a grand Scottish castle. As we park at last on the bank of a shallow river, opposite the lone house in the distance, Rebecca assures me her great-aunt is not titled, and she says the family isn't wealthy.

I give her a look.

"Well, *technically* I suppose they are," she says, getting out of the car and buttoning up her winter coat.

There are other cars parked here, which comes as a relief. I always find comfort in the presence of other people, especially when tucked away in the butthole of Britain.

"There's a lot of money in the land," Rebecca goes on, "if they were to sell. But the family's owned it for generations, bought it to farm it back when the land was cheap." She hands me her suit case and I shoulder my bag. The wind is frigid but I leave my gloves and scarf in my coat pocket, we'll be inside a warm house soon enough now. "But Great-Aunt Norah and Dickie were not farmers, and I don't think Dickie's parents were either. Norah rents the land to a tenant farmer for a pittance, and the house costs her each year. She has to keep it in a decent state of repair so we can spend Christmas here all together every year, but nobody has lived there since Dickie was a little boy, so it deteriorates quickly."

She stops abruptly and points to an oddly shaped metal bucket in front of us. "Luggage in there," she says.

I stare at her. "Why?"

"The house is still some way away, no need to break your back carrying our bags. It's much easier with the wheelbarrow."

Only now do I notice the wheel under the rusty bucket. "That's alright, I can carry the bags to the house." I'm not sure I'd be able to remove the rust stains if I shoved my suit case in there.

Rebecca sighs impatiently, then grabs the bags from me and throws them inside the wheelbarrow.

I seize the freezing handles and push after her. "Every time you come here," I say, "you have to make sure you've got over seventy miles' worth of petrol in the car. Talk about planning your trip! It's a logistical nightmare."

"And the closest petrol station is in Stradorroch, another twenty minutes up the main road. My dad used to always keep a can of petrol in the boot, just in case. Probably still does. His car's here, by the way."

An entirely different sense of dread fills me at the thought of meeting her father. There's nowhere to run if things go bad. We've only been together for six months. Is it too early to meet parents?

It takes me a few moments to realise we're walking away from the house. "Where are we going?"

"There." She points vaguely ahead. "How did you think we were going to cross the river?"

I can't see what she's pointing to. Only trees bordering the river, and intimidating mountains rising on both sides of the valley. "Isn't there a bridge somewhere?"

"*There*, you numpty. Don't you see it?"

Now I do. It is a bridge, I suppose, though not the kind I had in mind. It's a string of wooden planks held together by thin ropes, suspended over the river and tied around tree trunks on opposite banks. The whole concoction swings in the wind, and though the ropes turn out to be thicker than I thought as we get closer, my hands moisten around the wheelbarrow's handles despite the freezing gusts.

I step on the first plank and I'm surprised to see it holds my weight. I can't hear the wood creak with the screaming wind and the rush of the water below, but I can feel it under my foot well enough. There is a rope on either side at waist height to hold onto, but that's useless to me and my wheelbarrow. The wood beneath the wheel and my feet sways dangerously from side to side, and I've never been so scared of falling to my death. Twice I think of turning around and giving up, but how humiliating would that be? And where would I go, anyway?

"Don't worry, Tris, it's a perfectly solid bridge," Rebecca says after a quick glance behind her. "We've used it my whole life and no one has ever fallen over. Just think of the warm eggnog waiting for us when we get inside. Great-aunt Norah always has some ready to greet us."

I make it across the bridge dry and in one piece, and my heart settles down. We walk in silence as I take in the scenery. A clump of tall and straight pine trees to our left, with a large wood store, the logs piled all the way to the roof. A rather large axe is planted in a tree stump by the store, and a few stray logs are scattered over a bed of pine needles. A circular well stands to our right, the stones stained by time and neglect, and behind it a barn and an old tractor.

Something on the floor by the barn catches my attention. I put the wheelbarrow down and take a few steps away from the well-trodden path to have a better look. A row of mounds of freshly dug earth lines the cow shed. Rebecca stops too when she doesn't hear the squeaky wheelbarrow behind her.

"Is that...are those graves?" I ask. I get closer and...yes, the holes are perfect rectangles. I count thirteen of them.

Rebecca keeps quiet for a moment, then she gives a disbelieving laugh. "Norah has acquired a grim sense of humour. Either that, or Billy, the tenant farmer, is preparing to bury some animals."

But she doesn't sound convinced, and though I know nothing of the inner workings of a farm, I doubt farmers ever bury dead animals so close to a house. "How many will we be, in total?"

"Strip that look off your face," she scoffs. "You've watched too many films."

"How many?"

She takes a moment to count in her head. "Sixteen. Dangerously close, I'll admit. A creepy welcome for you, my dear." She gives a nervous laugh. She's being uncharacteristically awkward, which does nothing to reassure me. "Let's go have that eggnog, my nose is about to fall off."

The thought of a warm mug in my hands in front of a fire helps to shake off the feeling of creepiness, but as Rebecca opens the front door and announces her arrival, I sense that things aren't right.

No wave of heat to greet us, no smell of eggnog or mulled wine, and no jolly hubbub of Christmas music and family laughter.

A well-dressed man appears, hugs Rebecca, and says, "No sign of Mother, I'm afraid."

So I'll have to appease the sense of eeriness with a cold house, a smell of stale damp, and the terrifying prospect of meeting my girlfriend's father for the first time.

2

TILLY

Charlie glanced at the entrance hall. "I knew he was younger than her, about five years, right? But he looks even younger than that. A bit thin and lanky too, isn't he? She usually likes them bulkier."

I shrugged. Rebecca's new boyfriend wasn't unattractive, though he looked like he might bolt off any second. I couldn't blame him; imagine meeting this lot for the first time in this place.

I cast a quick glance behind me at Flynn, where he and his father were trying to get the newly sawn Christmas tree to stay up. His indifference towards me only made him more attractive, stupidly so. I kept reminding myself that the four years between us were nothing – my own parents had five years separating them – but at fifteen and nineteen it was *something*.

Flynn didn't care about me now, but one day, when I'm older, he might. And it wouldn't be *too* weird; we were just second cousins. Our fathers were first cousins, so surely, the DNA we shared was negligible. Charlie was my first cousin, and she felt much closer than Flynn did, despite being over a decade older than us.

Charlie handed me a larger log, and I placed it over the kindling sticks. "I wonder what held Granny up?" I asked.

"Who knows? And it's not like we can call her to find out. We'll just have to wait until she turns up."

"It's not the same without her here to prepare the house for us. It's cold and spooky when the fire hasn't been on and there are no decorations."

"You mean, you miss her telling you off for wearing those tights and getting another tattoo?" Charlie gave me a mirthless grin.

"I don't have any tattoos."

"No, indeed, that's only for my benefit. Don't worry, we'll make it as warm and cosy as usual, Granny or not. Lottie's making some mulled wine now, I can already smell it."

"I do like Mum's mulled wine."

I also liked Charlie's tattoos. I don't know what it was about her, but it suited her. Maybe the dyed blonde hair, or her general rebellious attitude. I wouldn't mind getting one, but it would just look silly on me. I wouldn't mind being like her at her age, if I could pull it off.

I placed a firelighter under the kindling as Dad entered the room.

"In case you were worried we'd get a break from Mum's nagging in her absence," Dad told everyone, "don't be, she's left us a note with instructions to play a game, because we can't possibly entertain ourselves without her."

"You're loving this, aren't you, Patrick?" Uncle Ellis, Charlie's father, said in a low voice, pacing on the edge of the room. "Spending Christmas without Mother."

"What kind of game?" Charlie said.

Dad ignored his brother's remark. He looked down at the note and said, "A sort of *True or False* game. She's prepared pieces of paper thrown into a hat and we pick them out at random, guess who it's about and whether it's true or not."

"Very Christmas-y," Charlie said, "nothing can go wrong here."

I couldn't help but agree. It seemed Granny wanted to make sure the traditional family drama happened with or without her.

"It'll be hard for you to join in the fun, Tristan," Dad said, "but you and Rebecca can team up. So, we've got our Christmas Eve activity sorted. At least it confirms Mother knew she was likely to be absent."

"Yes, but what happened?" asked Uncle Ellis. "She only said she may not be around when we arrive, and not to worry. But she made it here first, so why leave again and risk not being here for Christmas?" He shook his head. "It doesn't make any sense."

Uncle Ellis always kept decorum. He wore his impeccably white shirt just right, the collar coming out of the woollen jumper and immovable as if cut from glass, his cuffs carefully ironed, and not a greying hair stuck out of place. But his anxiety as to Granny's whereabouts stood out like a wrinkle on his shirt.

Dad was larger than him to start with, but without Granny's presence, he seemed even taller and wider. As if her absence allowed him to blossom.

We spent the afternoon going through the list of things Granny hadn't done. We got the house warm, made the beds, hung some dusty decorations, and brought more logs in to keep the fires going into the evening.

After an improvised dinner, Auntie Alicia organised everyone in the sitting room around the coffee table and log burner, Mum brought the rest of the mulled wine and some cups of tea, and I hovered on the outskirts of the sitting room, waiting to see where Flynn would seat himself. By the time he sat down on the sofa, however, he was sandwiched by Rebecca on one side and his father Killian on the other. I sat on the threadbare rug opposite him, separated only by the coffee table and therefore establishing a clear line of sight between us. The old wooden floorboards were cold and the equally old rug didn't do much to keep the cold away.

Nothing in this house seemed designed to keep it warm. A leaky flue and a poorly sealed plate meant draughts filled the inglenook fireplace. The windows' rotting wood allowed the wind in, and even the floorboards blew cold air. The sofas had been cold for so long it was like sitting on half wet half frozen fabric.

Tristan sat on the floor next to me.

"Someone should have told me to bring my ski kit," he told me in a conspiratorial tone.

"Yeah, sorry about that." I laughed. "Usually Granny is here before us to make the house warm. It takes a good few days to heat it, so we'll have a cold Christmas tomorrow."

He shrugged. "It would be fine if I could at least remember who is who. I've got Killian covered, but I can't remember a single other name."

"Frankly I think it's cruel of Rebecca to bring you here. If I ever have a serious boyfriend, there's no way I'm putting him through this."

"Well, serious is a big word."

"I'm Tilly." I placed a hand on my chest. "My parents are on that sofa, Patrick and Lottie," I pointed to the only couple not touching each other in one way or another. They loved each other, I knew that, but they weren't the type to be affectionate in public. "Next to Mum is Leon, Charlie's brother, and his wife Melissa." Melissa had her hand on Leon's thigh, but they were the opposite of Mum and Dad; I felt any attempt to show affection was forced and for display purposes only. I wasn't sure how they actually felt towards one another. "Then it's–"

"Kacey and Charlie," he cut in, "yeah, I remember meeting them. They're married, right?"

I nodded. "On the other sofa it's Violette, Charlie's mum, and her husband Ellis is…somewhere. I can't see him right now. Then it's Julian, he's my uncle by marriage, his wife Alicia is the Morrison, my dad's and Ellis' sister. She's the one standing up."

"She's the interim mother of the family, isn't she?" Tristan said.

I took a moment to think on that. He was right; she often took charge and she would probably take on the role of leader if Norah weren't here. Though Uncle Ellis liked to be in charge too, as the eldest. "Very insightful of you," I said. "And then–"

"Yeah I know the rest," he said. "Flynn, Killian, and Rebecca."

I leant in and whispered, "Killian is the son Norah wished she'd had instead of my dad."

"Right."

"Though I can't see why. Dad is hard working and became CEO, and Killian, well…"

He nodded understanding.

Auntie Alicia stood in front of the log burner with the upturned hat in her hands. "Ellis, what are you doing in the hallway?" she called out to her brother. "Come over here."

"He has been debating going to search for Norah," Auntie Violette said in her French accent.

"Oh don't be silly," Auntie Alicia told her brother. "You're not going to spend Christmas Eve away from your family on a wild goose chase."

Uncle Ellis reluctantly stepped into the room, his face heavy with concern. "I'm not playing this silly game."

"Oh go on," Auntie Alicia said, waving. "It's what Mum wants us to play and we've nothing better to do here. No telly, the damp got the board games, and we're too many to play cards. That's probably why Mum came up with this."

Uncle Ellis grumbled something and sat on the sofa's arm next to his wife.

"Right, let's start," said Auntie Alicia, and she plunged her hand into the hat. It came up with a piece of paper, which she unrolled and read, "One of us is handy with the strings–"

"Flynn!" shouted Charlie, and her wife Kacey nodded agreement.

My heartbeat was like a drum roll in my chest. My crush had first come to life when he'd played some guitar in this very room two years ago.

Flynn laughed, lifted his arms, and said, "Guilty. Though *handy* is a bit weak," he added with a grin.

"Right, so we can agree this is about Flynn," Auntie Alicia said, "the rest reads: and his dream is to one day travel the world as part of a boys band."

Laughter erupted in the room, and I probably laughed harder than I should have. Flynn and Charlie's debates on the merits of the

Backstreet Boys and One Direction and so forth had become family traditions.

"Do we have a consensus that it's false?" Auntie Alicia asked, and as everyone agreed, she threw the piece of paper into the fire. "Here's the next one: one of us wasn't born a Morrison but has been one of us longer than Charlie by ten years, longer than any non-Morrison, and was once a hairdresser."

All the heads in the room turned, and questions emerged. There were only three options – Mum, Auntie Violette, and Uncle Julian – but I didn't know which one had been married longest.

"It can't be Lottie," said Dad, "I remember introducing her to both Violette and Julian. It must be Violette, right? With Ellis being the eldest, and they married before Alicia and Julian did."

"But no," Violette said, "when I first met the family, Julian was already here."

"That's right," Dad agreed, "they were together a while before they married. So this is about Julian?"

"I suppose it must be," Uncle Julian said.

"Have we really been together longer than Charlie has been alive?" Auntie Alicia said.

"Impossible, we're not that old," said Uncle Julian, a glint in his eye.

"Oi!" shouted Charlie, followed by laughter. "By ten years it said, I'll remind you."

"Yes I suppose you first met the family in seventy-nine," said Auntie Alicia. "Here, as it happens. Like Tristan. And Charlie was born in eighty-nine."

"What about the second part," said Flynn with a grin. "Julian, a hairdresser?"

It seemed a far cry from his career as a paediatric surgeon, and I couldn't imagine him chit-chatting behind a chair.

Uncle Julian shrugged and crossed his arms. "I'm sure the game forbids me from giving any clues."

"No," said Dad, "I can't imagine him cutting hair. I say it's false."

"I don't know," said Lottie. "He *is* good with blades, isn't he?"

"Fair point," said Leon. "Julian's the type to excel at everything he does, so why not? Perhaps when he was young, before he decided to go into medicine?"

"Uncle Julian is funny," I said, "and he doesn't mind a good conversation, but I don't see him gossiping and talking about the neighbours with the local grannies."

"Well that's a stereotype and a half," said Auntie Alicia. "Not all hairdressers are like that."

I grinned. "Evidently Uncle Julian wasn't. I say it's true."

Killian let out a laugh. "Clever girl. I say it's true too."

I felt my chest glow, especially when Flynn's gaze finally fell on me following his father's comment.

Uncle Julian nodded. "That's right. In uni I worked as a hairdresser to help pay my way through. It was a fun part-time job, and it taught me some things."

"Right," said Auntie Alicia, "next: One of us can speak two languages fluently, and has never worked a day in her life."

The atmosphere darkened instantly. Smiles turned into awkward glances. I tensed up imagining what Tristan next to me must be thinking. "Anyone here is bilingual, other than Violette?" Auntie Alicia asked the room. I had always admired her ability to be superbly oblivious to cringey situations.

"No," said Uncle Ellis, "so we all know this is about Violette. Let's just move on to the next stupid riddle, shall we?"

"Hold on a minute," Killian said, "we've got to guess, it's the game. My guess is True."

"Killian," Uncle Ellis growled, "leave it."

"It's okay," Auntie Violette said, placing a hand on her husband's knee. "At least we know this game has Norah written all over it. Any other guesses?"

"You know what, I don't think it's true," said Auntie Alicia, and I thought she was only saying that to be friendly. As far as I knew, Auntie Violette was an old-fashioned housewife who had never seen the need to work since Uncle Ellis made a comfortable living as an accountant.

But I wasn't going to say so out loud. I was British, after all.

No one spoke after Auntie Alicia, and the awkwardness rose a notch. I avoided everyone's eyes, no longer just Flynn's.

"Granny needs to open her mind just a smidgen," Charlie said at last, and I was grateful. "Violette and all stay-at-home mums and housewives work every day with no days off, and no pay. I know it's a lot to ask of the elderly, but I hope none of you share her beliefs."

"Actually," Auntie Violette said, "it's false. I worked in a farm shop when I was in France as a young girl for a few years, before I met Ellis."

"There we go," said Alicia, "I think we can all agree I'm leading this game by a mile."

I thought this should end now; I could see what kind of mood Granny had been in when she wrote the game's content, but Auntie Alicia continued as if this was still fun.

"Next one: One of us likes attention, and would have spent more time behind bars had it not been for Leon."

If the atmosphere had been chilled with the previous riddle, it was positively frozen now. Only the crackling fire in the log burner and the wind whistling through leaky windows could be heard for a few moments, while everyone actively looked away from Charlie. I risked a glance at Tristan; he was staring at his feet.

This was a taboo subject. I didn't know enough about the circumstances which had led Charlie to a brief stay in prison some years ago to speak up. I assumed it was the same for everyone else here save perhaps for Kacey, Leon, and their parents – and Granny, apparently.

Charlie scanned the room and seemed baffled by everyone's behaviour. She gave a disbelieving laugh. "Is this what we all think, then?" she said. "Depraved Charlie landed herself in prison and almost dragged saintly Leon down with her. Is that it?"

She looked around, and I dared look back at her.

"Leon?" she said, fixing her eyes on her brother, sat awkwardly on a dining chair.

He reluctantly met her gaze, like a puppy about to be struck.

"Well?" she went on.

Leon shrugged, ever so slightly.

"Let's not go over this again, chérie," said Auntie Violette. "We know what happened, it's no use bringing it up again."

Flynn snorted. "Tell Granny that," he muttered.

Charlie let out a frustrated growl and stomped towards the door.

"Charlie," Dad said before she left the room, "if you want to talk about this, I'm always available." Then he gave the room an icy glare. "I think there's been enough judgement for one evening, don't you?"

If anyone was familiar with being misunderstood, it was Dad. I fought an urge to go to Charlie and comfort her, but I thought she might prefer to be alone right now.

"Yes, put the hat away, darling," Uncle Julian said, and Auntie Alicia did.

∽

They all sat there, sipping on tea or mulled wine, casting their line in the water every now and then in an attempt to start a conversation, but no one ever bit long enough to keep it going. Uncle Julian added a log on the fire. Killian whispered in his son's ear and Flynn rolled his eyes, Killian giggling like a naughty child. Tristan gripped his mug so tightly I wondered if it might slip out or break soon.

I looked at my phone; it was only eight, what else were we going to do with our evening? On Christmas Eve, of all nights? We couldn't just go to bed. If at least I had signal or wifi, I could waste time away on social media and texting friends. The tension made me so uneasy I could no longer stay still.

"I'm going to check on Charlie," I said as I got up.

I found Charlie coming down the stairs, on the way back to the sitting room. She looked downcast, her yellow hair limp on either side of her head.

"Are you alright?" I asked.

"I'll be fine."

"Are you sure you want to go back in already?"

She nodded silently. "Nothing new, is it? Thanks for checking up on me." She patted me on the back and looked around, as if searching for Kacey, but everyone was still in the sitting room.

By the time we returned, Auntie Alicia had gotten some presents out and was handing them to everyone.

I had completely forgotten about our tradition of giving each other a book on Christmas Eve.

"Why this?" asked Rebecca as she took one. "We usually receive only one each."

"Mum has decided to give everyone a book this year," Auntie Alicia replied. "I assume so anyway, they were all here and already wrapped when we arrived, with our names on them."

"See, Ellis?" Lottie said. "Norah knew she would likely not be here."

Uncle Ellis grunted and flattened a fold in his brown suit trouser.

Because it was so unusual, the books from Granny gained the most attention. "What did you get?" I asked Charlie.

"Gatsby," she replied and made a face. "I've read it and I already own two copies at home. You?"

I got a mystery novel I had never heard of: *Innocent Bystander* by C.A. Asbrey. I showed Charlie the cover. The back cover blurb sounded good, and it surprised me that Granny would get this right.

"What did Norah get you?" Uncle Julian asked Dad.

Dad turned the book over for Julian's benefit. It read *Warleggan*. "It's not even the first Poldark book, and I've never read any of it or watched the show. And she calls herself my mother. You?"

"*Crime and Punishment* by Dostoevsky."

"It's one of your favourites, isn't it?" Auntie Alicia said, stroking her husband's thigh affectionately.

Uncle Julian nodded. "Perhaps she knows me better than I thought, though if she did, she'd know I already have a copy, and this one isn't even a special edition. What did you get, darling?"

She took the book out of the wrapping and read out, "Robinson

Crusoe. I've never read it, so why not? Hardback too," she added, lifting her eyebrows.

"As always, favouritism," Dad said.

"Hang on, you don't know what Ellis got," said Auntie Alicia.

The book was on the coffee table, still wrapped, and Uncle Ellis did not look like he was about to pick it up anytime soon. Auntie Violette unwrapped it for him and read out, "*Inferno* by Dante Alighieri."

"You know," Auntie Alicia said, "I'm starting to think this is totally random. None of them really make any sense. What did she get you, Violette?"

"*Les Misérables*, which I've already read, in French *and* in English," she said, looking a bit peeved.

"And I see Killian got *A Storm of Swords*. That's one of the Game of Thrones books, isn't it?" asked Auntie Alicia.

Uncle Julian nodded.

"Poldark, Crime and Punishment, Game of Thrones, Les Mis, it's almost a selection of your favourite books," Auntie Alicia told him.

"Good point," Uncle Julian said, "so if anyone doesn't want their present, I'll happily rid you of them." He winked and it helped release the tension in the room.

When the mugs emptied and the fire started petering out, we made our way upstairs to the bedrooms.

"Anyone lucky enough to sleep on the second floor?" asked Flynn.

"Yep," Rebecca said. "Tristan and I drew the short end of the straw."

"We did too," said Uncle Julian. "With the gale out there, it'll feel like we're outside. I'm sure I saw an electric heater in the master bedroom. If it works, you can have it. I'm happy to use this as an excuse to have no choice but to keep my wife warm." He pinched Auntie Alicia and she giggled like a schoolgirl.

Mum, Dad, Auntie Alicia, and Uncle Ellis went up the creaky stairs to look at the second floor's rooms; I followed. The only working light in the master bedroom was a bedside lamp in one corner, and it cast a weak orange glow. The poor lighting and the mouldy walls gave the air a semblance of opacity, as if the darkness had materialised into a hazy fog. An abandoned bed stood against the wall, the metal rusted through and the soft furnishings streaked with fuzzy grey mould. In the room's corner opposite me, ropes and a piece of barbed wire hung from the ceiling; the room was in such a state it didn't even seem out of place.

"This is shameful," said Dad, gazing around with his hands on his hips. "How did we let this happen? We need to renovate the entire floor, or the rest of the house will follow."

"Let me guess," said Uncle Ellis, "you want to pay for it yourself? You haven't had enough opportunities to flaunt your wealth at us all those years, have you?"

Dad stared at his brother in silence.

"You know Mother can't afford it," Uncle Ellis went on, "and Alicia and I can't afford to throw tens of thousands at a house we only visit once a year. So obviously, this is only possible if you were to fund the project yourself."

I thought that was unfair and untrue; Alicia and Julian did very well for themselves, if not better than us.

"It's not just a house," said Dad, "it's the Morrison family house. It's been in the family for generations. We can't let it go to waste."

I wondered where this surge of family loyalty came from; he never tired of listing all the things that were deeply wrong with this family, and he debated every year whether we should come here for Christmas.

"In an ideal world, yes, we would build this place anew, even extend it, why not?" said Uncle Ellis, gesturing wildly. "But worldly limitations remain. Some of us do not have the means to indulge our every whim."

Patrick marked another pause, then said, "Never mind, Ellis. It was just a thought."

"Must you turn everything into an argument?" Auntie Alicia asked her brother. "Haven't you had enough of a lifetime of bullying? Leave Patrick alone for one bloody week. It's Christmas for God's sake."

I reflected on what was not being said. The emotionally abusive dynamics between Granny and her children, the jealousy, the envy, the death of Timothy.

Yes, Dad deserved to be left alone the only week they spent together every year. He and Mum had already suffered enough for a lifetime and more.

3

LOTTIE

Another long, sleepless night.

Whether I'm at home or not, the quality of my sleep remains the same. It seems I've never managed to get a good night's sleep ever since Timothy was born. At first it was the usual challenges of having a newborn, and then...

"Ready to go down?" Patrick asks.

He's standing by the door, his hand on the handle. I tell my feet to push off the floor but they won't obey. I feel like a deadweight, sinking further and further into the springy mattress.

"No," I say at last, because I'm not ready at all. Can't even begin to imagine seeing some of their faces, hearing the things that will be said, as they always are.

Patrick sighs and leaves the door. "What is it?" He hovers in front of me, his hands laced in front of his crotch.

"Why do you make me come back here every year? Isn't it agonising for you too?"

He shakes his head. "There's no point resisting it now, we're here and there's nowhere to go, so let's just get on with it, shall we?"

I purse my lips. I can feel the moisture gather in my throat, in my glands, and work its way up to my eyes, but I don't want to collapse again. I fight the tears, but it only distorts my face further. Now he feels awkward, I can tell. One hand furrows its way through his hair, the other lands on his hip, he shifts from one foot to the other. I don't want him to feel like this, but I can't help it. My mouth is claggy and salty.

"I've had enough of this lot," I manage to say in between heaves. "I want peace, Patrick."

Not that I'll ever get it, I'm well aware of that, but I want to try, and perhaps prove myself wrong. And as long as we keep seeing them, peace will only be a distant dream.

He sits beside me and wraps an arm around my shoulders. "Me too, darling."

That's probably the most intimacy we've had in months. I lean into him.

"Then why do we keep coming here?"

"I..." Another sigh. "I don't know. It's just something we need to keep doing. It won't bring Timothy back, but...I don't know."

I know what he means, even though I don't share the feeling. For him, I think, it keeps him alive, somehow. To be around family. Maybe I'd feel the same if I were a Morrison.

"Every time I see Ellis," I mutter, "and Killian, and Rebecca–"

"And Mum," Patrick adds.

I nod. "It grips me in the stomach, twists my gut. Still now, after all this time. How am I meant to keep putting on a friendly face? I don't know how much longer I'll last."

"I know, me neither. But it's not just them in the family. And that's another reason why we shouldn't drop off the face of the Earth; Tilly needs family, Charlie needs us, and Leon, Flynn, Alicia, Julian, they've got nothing to do with all this. I don't want to fall out with my sister."

"I would never ask you to cut Alicia out of your life, you know I wouldn't. But these reunions are taking their toll on me."

He drops a kiss on my hair. "We can reassess before next year, but it's Christmas today, and we're already here. Let's just get through it, okay?"

I nod, and he helps me up. As he moves to open the door, I grab his hand and he turns around. "Promise me that if it gets too intense, if Ellis or Killian or Norah stir trouble again and I get to a point where I can't take it anymore, we leave? We grab Tilly, jump into the car and go home?"

He marks a pause, then slowly blinks and says, "Fine, yes. I promise."

I wipe my eyes and cheeks, we walk out into the hallway, and meet Charlie and Kacey at the top of the stairs.

4

CHARLIE

I didn't sleep well. However much I tried to block it out, the Gatsby book stayed on my mind. It didn't only reflect Granny's perception of me, but everyone else's. She thought I'd enjoy the book because to her, to my parents, to my brother, I'm just like Jay Gatsby. Epicurean, obsessed with partying, drinking, giving in to debauchery and sensual pleasures. No morals, ethics, or brains. Never mind that I was a manager in my firm, that I was responsible for the company's entire social media strategy, and that I owned my house. To them, I would always be Charlie the irresponsible one.

I grouped them all in the same basket, but that was not fair. Alicia had always been the best auntie a niece could ask for, and Patrick and Lottie were the parents I should've had. Even now, as we were preparing a hearty Christmas breakfast together, we had a complicity I'd never felt with either of my parents. I broke the eggs above the hot pan and listened to the loud hiss.

"Oven," Lottie said, holding a tray of raw bacon in her mitts.

I stepped aside to let her open the door and take another tray of piping hot bacon slices out. "Oh, the smell," I said.

Patrick took a break from buttering his fleet of toast to stare at my eggs. "I would say I'm a decent-ish cook, generally, but I've never managed to get fried eggs right. They're always too cooked, brown at the edges, or too raw if I try to avoid this. How do you do it?"

"Ha, there is a trick to it. Do you use oil?"

He nodded.

"The same happened to me when I used to add oil. Now I just put butter in, wait for it to bubble, and then I add the eggs in and don't touch them until they look right. And they come right off."

He tapped the side of his head with his finger. "I'll remember that."

A modicum of respect. That was what was missing from my parents; I didn't feel they respected me. It would kill them to compliment me on anything, or show any type of affection. I supposed the lack of love was also at play, but I tended not to linger on this too much. Could prove painful, so I left it for the drunken nights, when I came back home and had Kacey's shoulder to cry on.

"How can I help?" Tilly asked, only just coming into the kitchen.

"The mimosa cocktails?" I suggested.

"Oy," came Kacey's voice. "That's my job. No one's preparing the tea, though?"

I took a second to take in the moment. This, right here, was what I longed for my entire life. The idea of a family gathering going smoothly, basking in the affection we held for each other, enjoying the simple things. A hot breakfast on Christmas morning, with no drama, no negativity, no judgement. Was it too much to ask for?

Apparently, yes. My parents came into the kitchen, followed by Leon and Melissa, and the temperature dropped instantly. We all said 'good morning' in the flattest tone, and the silence which followed swallowed any warmth which had been there before.

It didn't take a genius to figure what, or whom, the problem was.

"Happy Christmas. Everyone slept well?" Leon asked.

"Well enough," Lottie said, followed by a nod from Patrick.

Tilly shrugged, and Kacey replied with a perfunctory, "Yes, you?"

"Not too bad," Leon replied. "Charlie?"

I looked away from the hot pan for half a second and said, "Sure."

I had given him plenty of opportunities to be a good brother, to be a normal big brother, to make amends, and I was done trying. I would be civil – I was not one to create drama unnecessarily – but I wouldn't go out of my way to be friendly.

His stare lingered on me for a few seconds, then he moved on to the kitchen table.

"Dare I ask," Dad said, "any news from Mother?"

"Without a landline, signal, and post, it will be hard to get any news, won't it?" Patrick replied.

"No need for your sarcasm, Patrick."

"And I have no need for stupid questions."

My heart rate went through the roof. This was the story of my life; painful tension, and me stuck in the thick of it. I should side with my father, but I always felt closer to the people he argued with. He was always the unreasonable one, the prick.

I lifted some eggs with the spatula and dropped them on the toast Patrick had prepared, and though it was an innocent gesture, I felt like it was interpreted as a meaningful indication of whose side I was on. Though by now, at thirty, I think everyone knew where I stood.

Julian and Alicia walked in, and though they always lightened the mood and got along with everyone, even their cheery greetings failed to blow the cloud of tension away.

I couldn't help but think this breakfast was setting the tone for the rest of the day.

5

VIOLETTE

Christmas morning always brings mixed feelings. I loved it as a child, even though looking back, presents were miserable. I remember jumping around our house all day when I was eight because I'd gotten the doll I wanted. *One doll*, not even a nice one. Brittle beige strings of wool for hair, rough skin, a line of black thread for a mouth, the kind of thing that belongs in a horror film. Nothing else. No presents from other family members. Maybe it's a French thing, to receive only one present? But I don't think so, it must have been the times. Nowadays receiving just one present is unthinkable.

But as an adult the magic of Christmas wore off and it became a source of disappointment. Perhaps it's the result of having spent nearly all my adult Christmases with the Morrisons. Yet every Christmas morning I wake up with the remnants of the little girl's excitement in me, only to watch it dwindle to nothing over the course of the day.

I don't expect this year to be any different.

We've all taken a seat in the sitting room, on the sofa or on the floor, and Flynn is going back and forth between the tree and us, distributing the presents. The Christmas tree looks sorry for itself; we found some silver tinsel and a few wooden baubles, but no lights and there are far too few decorations for its size. The mountain of presents at its feet brings some much needed colour.

Leon is unwrapping one of our presents; Ellis originally objected to the price, but I reminded him that nothing is too expensive to show our son our love for him. Leon unfolds the Armani knit sweatshirt and beams at me. My heart is full.

"You shouldn't have," he says. "This is too nice."

He hugs me and drops a kiss on my hair, and this, right there, is the reason I had children. There is nothing better in life than making my boy happy. I glance at Ellis, but he's just as morose as he was last night, and that brings me back down.

Norah's absence is also weighing on me. It is too unusual, too odd. If she isn't here, then where is she? She can't be home alone, it's simply impossible. She has old friends and acquaintances in the area, of course, but would she spend the night there, on Christmas Eve? No, not if she could avoid it. The sun is piercing through the clouds outside and bringing the room to life, and it confirms the weather has been clement enough, if a bit gusty. She couldn't have been snowed in somewhere.

Charlie gives me a perfunctory hug for the mug I got her – not the type of embrace I'd expect from my daughter but there we are – but my mind is still with Norah. What we should be doing, is getting ourselves to the hospital to verify she isn't there, but no one else seems worried about her, and that is what is keeping Ellis and I from just storming off, I reckon.

If I didn't know this family better, I'd think they know what happened to Norah, and that's why no one worries. Perhaps they're *happy* she's not here. Could that be it? Surely not. The disrespect would be too much.

The pile of presents at my feet is getting rather large, so I grab the closest one. A bath bomb from Patrick and Lottie, and a quick look at the other presents confirms it's the only one from them. I've learned not to expect anything from them a long time ago, and in truth, I'm happy it's just a bath bomb. I've gotten them some fancy gardening gloves, one pair each. It's not really taking the high road, but something like it. The pinch of guilt I imagine they'll feel when they see the gloves and think of their 75p bath bomb is where I get my satisfaction.

I see the presents from Leon at my feet, the one from Charlie, and those from Julian and Alicia. I'd like to keep Leon's for last, so I put both presents from Alicia on my lap and carefully remove the tape from the wrapping paper.

A pair of slippers and a box of supermarket chocolates.

Is she having a laugh? I glance over to her, loud and cheerful as usual, perched on Julian's thigh, oblivious to my silent indignation. Her husband is a renowned surgeon, he makes hundreds of thousands a year, and all she can spare for her sister-in-law is *this*? What is the point of giving anything if they're going to make a farce of it? *Incroyable*. I am ashamed of the Molton Brown bath and body set I gave her, mortified when I think of the designer cashmere jumper that is waiting for her. I glance surreptitiously at the presents under the tree, still to be distributed, in case it's still there. Maybe I could sneak under and remove it. *I'll* bloody wear it. But I can't spot it.

I'm almost shaking; I can barely contain myself.

Leon sits next to me. "Everything okay, Mum?"

I force my lips to smile – ever so slightly – and nod. Bless him, we're so close he can feel my distress the second it comes over me, but I don't want to voice my frustration with everyone else around. "What did Patrick and Lottie get you?" I ask.

"Oh, a scarf," and he points to a rough-looking grey rag folded next to his unopened presents. It can't have cost them more than a fiver, and that's generous. Not that I'm surprised.

On cue, Charlie's gasp tears me away from Leon. She's holding a pair of boots in front of her, black leather lined with silver fur. She runs to Lottie and hugs her tightly.

The *gall* on her.

What did Leon ever do to Lottie, or Patrick? But of course, it has nothing to do with my son. They're doing it just to wind me up. I'd include Ellis in this, but he couldn't care less right now, so it's only for me.

I look around the room. Is no one else seeing this? The provocation is so obvious, how is no one commenting on the disparity between Charlie and Leon's presents? And then they say Ellis and I are the ones stirring up trouble in the family. Norah would say something if she were here. Of course she would.

I miss her all the more.

6

PATRICK

Forty-five years ago.
Patrick was ten years old, Alicia thirteen, Ellis sixteen.

Stairway to Heaven by Led Zeppelin.
    Patrick didn't particularly like the song, but Ellis did. It was his favourite, and the reason why he'd started learning to play the guitar in the first place. The reason Patrick didn't like it was probably because he'd heard his elder brother practice for months in the next room, and he simply could not play more than twenty seconds without going wrong.

Patrick had taken it upon himself to learn the tune, partly to show Ellis how to do it afterwards, and partly to gain his brother's admiration. If it meant so much to him, then surely he'd be impressed to see his little brother pull it off. He'd tried practising when Ellis was out, to make the surprise all the more special.

It hadn't taken long for Patrick to master the song. He loved music, and it came relatively easily to him. He'd played violin for five years already, and that was his true love. After his music teacher,

Harry, had told his parents he had a talent, his father had dusted off a violin he'd inherited years ago and given it to Patrick. It was not a particularly expensive or renowned make, but that violin was dearer to him than his life; old, delicate, yet so powerful. His teacher had ingrained in him the importance of taking good care of it, and Patrick had not allowed a single scratch to damage the polished wood ever since it had come into his possession.

One rainy Saturday morning, when Patrick felt comfortable enough not to mess up the song, he ran into his brother's room with the guitar in his arms.

"Don't have time," Ellis said, not even looking at him. "I'm going down."

"It won't take long," Patrick said, placing the guitar in position. His heart was pounding in his chest; he could barely contain his excitement.

When Ellis saw the guitar he went quiet.

When he heard him play without a single hiccup, his face dropped. Not his mouth like in the cartoons, but the skin on his cheeks sagged. He watched Patrick's little fingers glide along the strings, like a child seeing a live play for the first time. Then his eyes shifted to his younger brother's face, and Patrick understood in a flash that Ellis' reaction was not the one he'd expected.

He slowly let the tune die, and could not break the eye contact.

"Where did you even get a guitar?" Ellis asked.

"It's Alicia's, a present, but she never used it so she lent it to me."

"When did you learn to play?"

"Two months ago." Patrick gave him a bright smile. He knew that was quick, and he was proud.

"But...you don't even have a guitar teacher."

"I learned all by myself!"

A shadow passed over his brother's eyes. He grabbed his wallet off his desk. "Congratulations," he muttered as he walked past.

Patrick stood in Ellis' room for a few moments, alone, wondering what had happened.

THE FOLLOWING TUESDAY, Patrick spent the first hour after school looking for his violin all over the house. He wanted to practice for his lesson on the next day, but it wasn't where he'd left it.

He found it at last outside, by the backdoor, out of sight behind a wall. The case was open, and it was raining.

It had been raining non-stop since Saturday, and it was February. The cold, dampness, and moisture had already done its irreversible damage. The wood was warped, the strings had rust stains. Patrick stood in the rain for a moment, unbelieving. He wanted to cry, but the tears didn't come to his eyes. He knew it was Ellis; it wasn't the first time he'd stolen or broken his favourite toys. But this was different; he had tampered with his greatest passion. It was not a toy, it was…a part of him. If Ellis had broken his arm, it would have been less painful.

By the time he'd brought the ruined violin back inside, he wanted to murder Ellis. He found his mother in the kitchen. "Look what Ellis did," he said, holding the wreck of a violin in his arms.

She cast a sideways glance, then returned her attention to the potatoes she was peeling. A wave of dread washed over Patrick's body. Did his mother already know about this?

"It's ruined!" he complained. "He left it outside in the rain, Harry always said that a little bit of moisture could damage it forever. This is *completely* ruined."

Tears came to his eyes, not only because of his violin, but because he could see the words weren't getting to his mother.

"It's your own fault for not looking after your possessions, Patrick," she said, and shrugged. "If you'd noticed sooner, you might have been able to retrieve it in time."

Patrick was gobsmacked. He stood there, dripping wet, and felt stupid. "I want a new one," he said at last.

His mother laughed. "Your dad inherited this one, these things cost a fortune. You're not getting a new one."

The tears streamed down his cheeks. Did she mean it?

When she saw his face, she shook her head and raised her eyebrows. "Let it serve as a life lesson. If you don't look after your things, there is a price to pay."

"But it's Ellis who did it!" he shouted louder than he wanted.

"Blaming other people won't make you look good." She returned to her potatoes.

"I love it, I am good at it, I don't want to stop!"

"Nobody likes a boaster either. Vanity does not become you. Learn to be humble. Take it on the chin, Patrick."

"It's so unf–"

"Now quit pestering me and get out of my way," and she walked past him to throw the potato skins into the bin.

7

JULIAN

Patrick stands next to the smallest pile of presents, and Julian feels sorry for him. He convinced Alicia to get him a rally racing experience which cost them an arm and three fingers, but that's just an envelope, and the rest of his Christmas plunder looks miserable as a result. He knew he couldn't count on Ellis or Norah or Killian to contribute. But then he remembers Patrick is a big boy, with a big job and wealth which must tower over his, and he recovers quickly enough.

To say he has other things to worry about would be an understatement.

He helps clear up the tornado of wrapping paper, piles it inside recycling bags, and smiles when Alicia kisses him on the cheek to thank him for her present, but he can't give her his full attention, not as much as he'd like, anyway. He wants to savour the moment, and knows he should; if he could only be in the present, this would be perfect.

People are trying their new clothes on, setting up gadgets, generally playing with their presents in good humour, and Tristan must think this is a merry family on the jolliest of holidays. The smell of lunch cooking has overcome at last the house's musty odour of abandonment, and now that the fire has been roaring for several hours, it's positively nice and toasty. He can even detect a hint of pine wafting off the Christmas tree and blend in with the turkey's fumes. Julian never liked Norah anyway, so he reckons they can all get along while she's away. Well, to an extent. Violette and Ellis would need to leave for everyone to get along.

But Julian's internal struggle keeps his mind away from the present moment, and though he's doing his best to keep it concealed from his wife, he isn't sure she isn't suspecting something. So he keeps himself busy in order to deprive his face from betraying him.

"Wouldn't it be a good idea for Ellis and Violette to go looking for Norah?" he asks Patrick and Lottie as they're helping him clear the floor. He hopes they understand what he's trying to do here.

"No," comes Alicia's voice from behind. "Not yet."

Her tone brooks no argument, so Julian submits to his wife. He doesn't usually go against her wishes, and he certainly won't start now, of all times. He exchanges a look with Patrick.

Why does she want to keep those two around, though? He knows she feels the same as he does, that they're grumpy buggers who will not allow anyone to have a good time. Not to mention their presence always brings the elephant with them.

His own issues come back to the fore and he returns his attention to shoving the wrapping paper into his bag, mechanically, like an automaton.

8

TRISTAN

Alicia brings in the glowing turkey and I have to give it to them; they know how to cook a Christmas dinner. The food was brought fresh yesterday so it's miles from the measly dinner of tins and crackers we had last night, which Norah would normally have been in charge of preparing.

There was an argument over the seating arrangement prompted by Ellis – though it looked to me that Violette was silently pulling the strings and she may have incited her husband to talk for her – but it is forgotten now. As long as I have Rebecca on one side, I don't mind who sits on the other. It turns out to be Flynn, my would-be brother-in-law in some very, very distant and theoretical future.

The dishes stream past me in succession, each furiously awakening my senses: steaming peas in butter, pig-in-blankets, roasted potatoes, boiled cabbage, golden Yorkshire puddings, moist turkey breast slices – Julian and Charlie have already claimed the thighs –, roasted parsnips and carrots, and so on.

The wine flows because we've got nowhere to go, and there's a liberating feeling about the notion of being...stuck, for want of a better word, in such a remote place. It gives everyone licence to drink liberally, and for a little while, it results in a gay atmosphere.

"I think we need some music," Alicia says. "Is there a speaker or CD player here somewhere, or should we just use a phone?"

"I've got a bluetooth speaker upstairs," Charlie says. "And I suggest we play my playlists because..."

She eyes Flynn sideways with a humorous expression on her face.

"What is that supposed to mean?" Flynn says.

"Well, we have...how shall I put it...*different* tastes, don't we? And I think the good Morrison family would enjoy some quality music."

Flynn taps the edge of the table with both hands. "I agree, I'll get my phone straight away."

The entire table erupts in laughter. This is the first time it happens since I've met them.

Flynn doesn't actually stand up to get his phone, says he was joking, and Charlie leaves to fetch the speaker. By the time she returns, however, the mood has already changed.

"I'm not hungry," Ellis says, pushing away his plate still piled high with food. "I can't eat while we still don't know what happened to Mother. Can you?" He's asking the entire table.

I suspend my fork halfway between the plate and my mouth. It's loaded with turkey breast, peas, and gravy, and I really want to shove it in my mouth.

"Do you want to throw all this food away, then?" Patrick asks.

"No, course not," and he gives a dismissive wave of the hand.

Relieved, I munch on my forkful.

"But it's wrong to be laughing and eating merrily on Christmas Day without her here," Ellis goes on. "I've not done it since I spent Christmas in France with Violette's family a good fifteen years ago. And certainly never here, in this house."

"I know, it's awful," says Alicia. "It's on my mind too, of course it is." Though I notice she keeps on eating. "I wasn't too worried yesterday because I just assumed she'd be back today."

"It's too strange," Killian says. "It's not like her. I couldn't get any sleep last night."

"At which point do we leave the estate to get phone signal and make some calls?" Julian asks.

"Who would you call, though?" Killian asks. "It's not like she's got a mobile." He chuckles, but my dislike for him grows. Even I can think of several calls to make.

"Billy, for one," Ellis says. "He's our closest neighbour and the one most likely to know something. And then the hospital, the police station."

"And Margaret," Alicia says. "Mum said she might pay her a visit, which is where I'm hoping she is. Perhaps she had a car problem and she couldn't let us know."

"It would help if this house had a bloody landline," says Charlie. "What a thing to say, in the twenty-first century."

"To answer Julian's question," Lottie says, and her husband Patrick nods with his mouth full next to her, "I think we should consider going for a drive by late afternoon if we still don't have any news."

"I might go now," Ellis says.

"Please, Ellis," Alicia says. "Stay for dinner, and then charades. Then you're free to go and ruin the rest of Christmas."

"Charades? I don't think so."

But in the end he does stay for charades. It's hard to play this game without laughing and bathing in a playful atmosphere, so I look forward to recreating the glimpse of family fun I saw earlier. I'm also hoping it will help pass the time quicker.

We are divided into teams of three and four, and I end up with Rebecca's immediate family. The more I get to know Killian the less I warm to him, yet I still feel the pressure of wanting to be accepted by him. I may not like him, but I want him to like me. So I see charades as an opportunity to bond, and I'm hoping luck will be on my side.

The only problem is, I've only played charades twice in my life, and I suck. Not only do I seem to always pick titles I've never heard of, but when I do pick something I know well, I'm rubbish at acting it out. How in hell do you act out the film *Gone With The Wind*? Even worse, over the two hours we play the game, I guess only once correctly – and many times when it isn't our team's turn, naturally. So when the last round comes, Julian, Alicia, Charlie, and Kacey's team leads by a mile, and we compete neck-to-neck to avoid last place with Ellis' team. Alas, Killian is a very competitive chap; he will *not* accept last place.

And whose turn is it to stand in front of everyone? Yours truly. I pick *The Sound of Music*, dance around trying to convey I-don't-know-what, make involuntary noises as I sing the melodies in my head and am told off for breaking the rules, and generally humiliate myself as time runs out and neither Killian nor Rebecca nor Flynn have a single clue as to what I'm doing up there. I can't look at them as I recover my seat next to Rebecca, too ashamed to have let Killian down. On Ellis' team, Leon guesses correctly when Violette performs *Romeo and Juliet*, and we lose.

Julian claps loudly from the kitchen to celebrate his team's win, and Alicia brings out the losers' traditional punishment: four full mugs of eggnog, loaded with brandy.

"I'll sit this one out," says Killian moodily. "Not a fan of eggnog. I'll gladly down a pint of mulled wine instead, if you like?"

"Not a chance," says Alicia, handing me my mug. "What kind of punishment would it be, if you could choose your drink? Go on."

Killian grunts and gulps the entire mug's contents in frustration. We all exchange an amused look; Killian is quite the character.

I'm bringing the mug to my lips when a loud gurgling noise emerges to my right. I stop abruptly, the eggnog spills but is drowned out by the sound of Killian's mug shattering to pieces on the hardwood floor.

His hands are gripped tight around his neck. His face has gone from red to dark purple in just a few seconds, the whites of his eyes bulging out of their sockets. He foams at the mouth, drops to his knees, collapses to the floor, writhes a few more times, then goes limp.

Rebecca and Flynn are all over him, turning him onto his back, shaking him, slapping his cheeks to extricate a sign of life. Alicia puts her hands over her mouth and screams. Everyone else is frozen into space, eyes glued to his lifeless body.

To say that a few moments ago I was worried about hurting his feelings...

I will never have to worry about that again.

9

LOTTIE

"There's nothing we can do," says Julian, bent over Killian's chest. He's the only medical person in the family, and as a surgeon, if he can't do anything, then it's final. His words bring a shock to the room, and for a long time I can't move. It makes it real. Has Killian really just died, in front of us? A few moments ago he was grumbling as a sore loser, and now he's dead?

It feels like my muscles atrophy, as if the control over my own limbs is leaking away, and the detail which sends a chill down my spine is that the feeling is familiar. Nineteen years ago, my body initially responded in a similar fashion. The emotional shock has an existing pathway to follow, as it manifests itself physically.

"Was there a lump in the drink?" asks Kacey.

Alicia is struggling to bring herself to speak; her face is contorted and her hands are glued to her mouth. She shakes her head several times. "Nothing large enough to do this." Her voice is muffled.

"Do we know of any allergies he had?" asks Julian.

Heads turn to Killian's children. Violette is hugging both, though they seem reluctant to lean into her. "I don't think he had any, did he?" Violette says.

"No," says Flynn, his face impassive. "Just hay fever."

"But he very rarely drinks eggnog," Ellis points out. "Perhaps there's something, a spice, or the brandy, that doesn't sit well with him, and drinking the entire mug in one go may have been too much."

I look at Julian; he doesn't seem convinced, but keeps quiet. I suppose if he doesn't have a better explanation, it's no use shooting plausible theories down.

My hand reaches to Tilly's, and I draw her against me. I'm not letting her out my sight.

"What do we do now?" asks Leon. He doesn't know what to do with himself; he wanted to comfort Rebecca and Flynn but Violette and Tristan were quicker, and now he's standing awkwardly next to his wife, wringing his hands together.

"We need to call an ambulance, or the police," says Charlie, "to get him to a hospital. They'll determine the cause of death and do… the rest."

"But how?" asks Patrick. "There's no signal."

"We'll just have to drive," I say. "Get to the nearest police station or hospital. Which is closest?"

"And leave Dad here?" asks Rebecca, her voice hoarse.

"I think we have to, for now," I reply.

"The police station in Stradorroch is closer," Ellis says. "I'll go."

He's probably hoping he'll find a trace of his mother while he's out. Our silence signals our agreement. He leaves the room, and we stand frozen in grief and shock around the corpse of a man who still had so much to live for.

About ten minutes later, Ellis comes rushing back into the room. "My car has no more petrol," he says, panting. "I know for a fact I had half a tank left when we got here yesterday, I don't understand. We have to use another car."

We all go outside, leaving Violette with Rebecca and Flynn to look over Killian. It's only late afternoon, but night has already cast its dark blue veil. The wind is raging, as it always seems to be at this time of year. If only there was snow, at least it would feel more Christmas-y, but then we wouldn't be able to leave by car.

We cross the swinging bridge, and Patrick tries to turn the car on. It sputters and coughs but won't ignite. I look at him through the window; he's genuinely puzzled, and keeps trying and trying, in vain.

"There's petrol all over the ground," says Tilly. She's turned her phone's light on and is staring at her feet.

I crouch down and with my finger I brush a wet stone. I bring the finger to my nose and balk at the nauseating smell. "Yes, definitely petrol," I say, standing back up.

Two more cars sputter, but won't start.

"Rebecca said her father always keeps a can of petrol in the boot of his car," said Tristan.

"Yes!" exclaims Alicia. "He does." She rushes to Killian's old jeep. I'm relieved when the boot opens; I thought the car might be locked.

The can of petrol is there, red plastic under a layer of black dirt. Alicia lifts it but instantly groans. "Empty," she says.

I'm not letting go of Tilly's hand. I don't like this. I don't like any of it. And I'll be damned if I'll let anything happen to a child of mine ever again.

"My car has a locked petrol cap," says Charlie, and strides over to it.

She jumps into the driver's seat, turns the ignition, it coughs a few times then roars and ignites. I never thought an engine's low rumble could fill me with so much joy. I realise, in this moment, that getting help is no longer just about Killian; the tanks didn't empty themselves, so we need the police to know about us.

"Go," says Julian, "go to the police station. Tell them what is going on."

Charlie nods and closes the door. She puts the gear into reverse, the engine still purring nicely, but as she weaves her way out of the parking area, the car leaves a wet thread behind it, and the engine coughs a couple of times before stopping altogether. Charlie tries to restart it a few times, but it won't catch and she gives up.

The sudden silence brings with it the stench of doom. My

muscles tense and my entire body dries up. My pulse quickens. I sense the presence of darkness, of evil, like a floating spirit breathing in my ear, calling to me, taunting me. As if I'm standing in the chilling trail of the devil's own passage.

In a flash, I find myself nineteen years earlier. Back in the house on Elm Street, standing on my doorstep. The front court is empty, devoid of sounds, of Timothy's singing, of his playful shouts, of the scraping of the tractor's plastic wheels on the gravel and tarmac. A car in the distance picks up the speed in a jolt of acceleration. The weight of the world collapses onto my chest as I understand my son, my only child, has been taken.

I inhale, and it's like breathing in thick smoke. For a moment I can't move; I just feel the air, the threat in the wind, the evilness all around. Just a fleeting moment before I start moving and scramble for a phone, then sob when Patrick answers at last.

That moment, I am feeling it now, as I stand frozen in the middle of the Scottish Highlands, the wind whistling and whirling around me. *It's* back. But this time, the moment lasts longer; it takes a while before I can move again.

As if the darkness is here to stay.

10

JULIAN

"We can't leave the corpse in the house, especially if we don't know when we'll be able to get help," says Julian. "Soon the putrefaction will make it too unhygienic to keep indoors." In addition to the excretion of other fluids, but he didn't see the need to mention it.

They all hover in front of the house, pushed around by the gale and forced to shout to make themselves heard, as if entering the house would be an infraction, or synonymous with danger.

"There is a ready-made hole there," Tilly says, pointing behind Julian and where the barn stands. "Regardless of what it was initially dug for, it makes it convenient now."

"No," Lottie says firmly. "It would feel wrong. Nobody here knows who dug those holes, and for what purpose. What if this is part of the killer's plans?"

It surprises Julian to see several faces light up, as if understanding only now that someone may have pre-arranged everything. Tilly is one of them, and she stares wide-eyed from Lottie to the row of holes and back.

"What are the options?" Patrick asks Julian. "Where else could we store a corpse?"

"The barn," Julian says, "or the cellar perhaps."

"The barn doesn't feel right," says Alicia. "Wouldn't rats get to it? Though I suppose the cellar wouldn't be any different. Oh, poor Killian," and her voice dies in a string of sobs.

"The priority is to preserve the body so that the cause of death can be determined when we do get help," says Julian, "but I admit I can't think of a good location for this, other than somewhere cold."

He doesn't know if there is any point in preserving the body, as immediate help is not available and by the time an expert examines the corpse, any trace of the poison will likely be gone. For he knows Killian has indeed been poisoned; the symptoms, and the quickness of it, left no other option. He kept that fact to himself in the sitting room in order not to create a sense of panic, and there is no point mentioning it now either; even though criminal intent has since become evident, there is no use bringing the panic level up a notch by pointing out that Killian has in fact been murdered in front of them. They may be aware of it subconsciously, or in the safety of their mind, but mentioning it out loud will make it real and no one would benefit from it.

In the end, they decide to bury the corpse in the ready-made grave-shaped hole, but not without grumbling.

"I don't like it," says Lottie as she watches Julian, Patrick, Ellis, and Leon drop the body and then shovel the loose earth on top. "Feels like we're cooperating with the person behind this. Like we're doing their bidding and willingly being manipulated."

"But *who* are you talking about?" asks Tilly. "It's only us here."

Lottie exchanges a glance with Patrick, and it starts a chain reaction of silent but meaningful looks. The atmosphere shifts to open suspicion. Tilly seems to realise what everyone else is thinking, she looks at Julian who presses his lips together to confirm her suspicion, and she doesn't blink for a while.

The shovelling resumes and, when the hole is filled to nearly ground level, they all make their way back inside the house.

"I'll stay outside a while longer," says Flynn. "I need some time alone."

"I don't know, Flynn," says Charlie. "It's not safe. We should stick together."

"I'll be fine," the teenager says in a tone which brooks no argument, and he walks away.

They avoid the sitting room, where shards from Killian's mug still lie under the coffee table and sofa. They choose the dining room, Ellis sits at the head of the long table, and he calls for silence.

He seems to have recovered some composure. Following the news of Norah's absence, he shut himself away and refused to engage more than the strict minimum. Now, colour has returned to his face, and there is purpose in his eyes. He's recovered his leading role as the family's eldest member after Norah.

Julian pops a mint into his mouth and offers one to Alicia, but she shakes her head.

"I believe there is no more doubt as to the suspicious circumstances surrounding Mother's disappearance," Ellis says, and looks around the table. When no one objects, he goes on. "There is someone behind our stranding and her absence. Someone clearly wants to harm us, and they may have already harmed Mother."

His voice wavers when he says that last word, Julian notes. He clearly deeply cares for her, however unhealthy the relationship.

"We must explore every single avenue available to us to get help," Ellis goes on. "The cars are no longer an option, unless someone knows of a hidden can of petrol anywhere on the property?"

"The tractor?" asks Tilly.

"Already checked," says Patrick, and he shakes his head. "Empty."

"What about Billy?" asks Leon. "Can we reach his house on foot? He's the closest neighbour, after all."

Ellis winces. "Doubtful, too far away, especially in this weather. Even if we cut across the land, as the crow flies it will be a good ten, fifteen miles, with some climbing to do and a river to cross. Maybe more than once."

"But our survival is on the line," Charlie says.

"You're probably more likely to die on that hike than by staying here."

"Here, while we wait to die?"

"Let's calm down," Alicia says. "There will be no more deaths, God willing. It's a matter of getting help to do what's right by Killian, and having a means to leave and go back home once our week here is over."

Oh, Julian thinks, gazing lovingly at his wife. Is she really so naive?

"And finding Mother," Ellis reminds her with a stern look.

"Yes," Alicia says, "though I'm still not entirely sure how that's related."

"Someone will come eventually," Patrick says before Ellis can reply. "We've got electricity from the turbine, wood for heating, water from the river, the kitchen and pantry are full of food. Billy is our land's tenant farmer, he's sure to come at some point to look after the livestock, and he'll have to use the barn and tractor sooner or later."

"It's the holidays," Julian points out. "He may not come here for a week or two."

"Farmers don't have holidays, the livestock still needs to be looked after," Charlie says, "but even if Billy does come, the cattle is far enough that he may be able to do his job without ever coming close to the house. I don't remember seeing any cow or sheep in the last ten or fifteen minutes of driving on the way here."

"Waiting passively doesn't seem right," says Lottie, her hands resting on Tilly's shoulders. "By the time someone comes to one of the most remote locations in the country, another one of us might be dead."

"Why would anyone want us dead?" asks Alicia. "Is anyone here part of an organised crime group that we don't know about?" That's an attempt at lightening the mood, but it falls flat. Julian takes her hand in his, and keeps sucking on his mint. He feels the mint is inappropriate for the situation, but it helps him keep his cool.

"Take your head out of the sand, Alicia," says Ellis. "Killian's death is mightily suspicious, we have no bloody idea where Mother is, and someone *physically* emptied all of our cars' petrol tanks. Including the tractor's, for God's sake."

Alicia's fingers tighten around Julian's hand; perhaps it's sinking in at last. Her other hand places a lock of hair behind her ear, and repeatedly pulls on it; a sign she's nervous.

"There are fourteen of us here," says Lottie, "between us we must cover all phone towers. Have we all double checked that we have no service at all? I don't, I've looked several times, both outside and in."

There's a rustle as everyone takes their phone out and check. All the heads shake, and Julian knows this is futile. Over the years, no one has ever reported having signal, not as far as he can remember.

"We'll have to go outside in the morning and check if we get signal in different locations," Lottie goes on. "We only need one call to go through, it could make all the difference."

"Is there a bicycle here?" asks Leon, and that's a good point, Julian thinks. Leon is an accomplished cyclist and would be able to cover the distance to the closest police station.

"I seem to remember seeing one a few years ago," says Ellis, "but it was in bad shape. I think it had been there for so long the metal was rusty and the tyres were ruined."

"Yes," Leon says, "if it's been too long the rubber will lose its elasticity and crack. It's worth a look, though. Where is it?"

"The barn's hayloft, I think. Or the attic, I remember it being dark and dusty."

"I'll have a look as soon as we're done here."

Alicia squeezes Julian's hand again, in hope this time. His gaze falls on her, and his heart cries out for her. If there's a silver lining, it is that these events are distracting him from his own woes. If only she knew that even if they come out of this alive, their problems will be far from over. The weight of his issues almost make the current situation look like child play. He wishes he could spare his wife the misery to come, but it's too late now. Back home, it will all come crashing down. He's glad both their sons are abroad and will not have to witness any of it.

"I don't suppose anyone here has, or has seen, some type of red flare like they use at sea?" asks Rebecca, eyes puffed and red, coming out of her silent grief. "It might attract attention, cause someone to come and check why it was fired?"

"Yes, yes," replies Ellis, "I mean no, I don't believe we have any, but that is a very good idea. We could create some smoke in daylight, some black, some white, several plumes, and someone somewhere is bound to see it and wonder what in the world it is."

"But we are in the middle of a ten thousand-acre estate," Patrick says. "And in a valley, surrounded by mountains. It's quite likely no one will see it."

"What do we have to risk?" asks Lottie. "We have to force our luck, to do things which may lead one person to become concerned, and it won't happen if we mope here all day, jumping at every gust of wind."

"What I mean," Patrick replies, "is that getting external help seems unlikely, so we will have to rely on ourselves. I think I'm speaking for everyone when I say that the person who emptied the petrol tanks can't possibly be one of us."

All heads nod, save for Ellis', Julian notes. He's studying his brother with intent.

"So if it's someone else," Patrick goes on, "they must be outside, hiding somewhere. In daylight we must search the grounds, inspect anything that could serve as shelter, look for any sign of life, of someone trying to keep themselves warm."

Leon winces. "Quite unlikely though, isn't it? It's winter, the wind is brutal. The only safe refuge for miles around is this house."

"Don't underestimate what some people can withstand," Patrick says. "The barn would be perfectly adequate. A cave of some sort, a hole in the ground, a shed or ruin we may have forgotten about. As long as they are sheltered from the rain and most of the wind, and they have enough layers to keep warm, it's entirely feasible."

"But there are no caves on the estate, nor sheds, or ruins we don't know about," Ellis says.

"Have you checked the ones we do know about?" Patrick asks curtly.

Ellis keeps silent.

"Then you don't know. We'll check them in the morning. As for caves, can you really say with conviction there are no caves in, say, a mile radius around the house?"

"Yes, absolutely," replies Ellis. "Unlike you, I've visited this house more than once a year for Christmas. I've kept an eye on everything. As boys, while you played violin and buried yourself in books, I was scouring every inch of these lands, and if there was a cave anywhere, trust me, I would know."

The front door shakes the house as it slams shut, and loud steps thump across the hallway. Alicia's eyes shoot to Julian, and he can feel the entire room tense.

Then Flynn appears in the doorway, and everyone relaxes – but only for a second.

He catches his breath, then says: "I've found Norah's car."

11

ALICIA

I was torn. The mad turn of events was tearing me from the inside, my anxiety like a winch stretching my nerves to the point of breaking. At the same time, I couldn't help but feel relieved that my two boys weren't here this year. My heart had filled with sadness when they'd independently announced they wouldn't be returning to England for the holidays this year. It was the first time I'd spend Christmas without either of my sons. I hadn't told them; there was no point making them feel guilty for living their lives. Now, however, I couldn't believe my luck. The worst case scenario was not the *worst* case scenario. I couldn't imagine what state I'd be in if this happened with my boys here; no wonder Lottie didn't leave Tilly's side ever since the petrol debacle.

Flynn jogged along the track with his phone's light held in front of him and everyone else followed him at a fast walk, save for Ellis who ran too, close behind the teenager. It was a sight; I couldn't think of a single time I'd ever seen Ellis exercise. He avoided it so much it was as if he believed sweat would permanently stain his sacred shirts. Yet now, he had no care for his appearance. His glasses were wonky, his thinning hair dishevelled, his shirt half tucked inside his suit trousers, the other half hanging haphazardly around his waist and flowing in the wind. He'd have a heart attack if he saw himself.

Flynn veered off the driveway and led the pack into wet tall grass, where my own light uncovered tyre tracks. And then I saw it, Mum's fifteen year-old Vauxhall Astra, tucked under the lip of a steep bank and beneath a leafless tree. I was petrified of what we'd find inside. Would Mum be there? And if so, alive? The blood pulsed in my ears, and my mouth dried up.

Flynn's light momentarily fell on Mum's haggard face inside the car, the top half of her head covered in a black cloth and her mouth open as if gasping for air. My heart fell inside my chest. Relief at finding her alive never checked in; that fraction of a second was enough to convey the torture she had gone through.

Ellis cried out, losing all decorum and forgetting himself. His face contorted in anguish and he pushed Flynn out of the way to throw the car door open himself. In a few seconds Mum was out of the car, held in Ellis' embrace. I hugged her too, then hastily removed the cloth covering her eyes while Ellis untied her hands and feet. The black cloth had been taped onto her skin and hair, and when I removed it from her face, it left a neatly delineated red raw mark on her skin. Her eyes struggled to open because of the phones' lights. Her face's skin was a lifeless grey, more wrinkled than used foil, and sticky from the dried sweat. She reeked of urine and faeces, and that was enough to ensure she wasn't crowded by the relatives.

"Oh Granny," said Charlie, "what happened?"

Mum opened and closed her mouth a few times, unable to make a sound. She looked like a lost rabbit, unsure of where she was, or what was happening. I had never seen her so drained and gaunt.

"Leave her alone for now," Ellis said in a dry tone. "She needs to recover and have a wash before she can tell us what happened. Can you walk, Mother?"

She gazed at the ground, her feet, the lights, she squinted, then opened her mouth one more time soundlessly. Ellis carefully lifted and pivoted her into his arms, and I was glad, rather selfishly, that I wasn't in his shoes. I was also thankful for the darkness which concealed the evidence of Mum's soiled clothing.

Ellis walked on ahead of everyone else, and by the time I entered the house, he and Mum were already locked away in a bathroom. The wait for her to come out and explain what had happened was unbearable. The rest of the family whispered to each other, speculating away, but I was unable to bring myself to do or say anything. Julian tried to be affectionate but I turned away, needing to be left with my thoughts. I was scared, angry, and sad all at once. Who would do something like this to an eighty-three year-old defenceless woman? How long had she been in that car for, in the middle of the Scottish winter? It was all I could do to keep the questions inside, but there was no use voicing them until Mum was back.

When Ellis brought her down to the dining room, she looked a different woman. Different from the helpless and haggard victim we'd found in the Astra, but a hundred percent the Norah we all knew. She wore a clean gown over green wool tights, soft slippers on her feet, and her thin white hair had been combed backwards. The haughty, condescending glint in her eye had returned, much to my chagrin. She held herself straight – or as straight as her aged back would allow – and the ancient pride inhabited every part of her body. The red marks left by the tape on her cheeks had faded to pink lines, and she had dark purple bags under her eyes, but other than that, it was as if she'd never been held captive in potentially fatal conditions.

Ellis pulled a chair at the dining table for her, and she sat down like a lady attended by her manservant. She was acting even more dramatic than usual, if that was possible. She stared everyone down as if they had personally offended her. I thought I'd jump to her side as soon as she'd be out of the bathroom, gripped by a burst of empathy for the torment she had endured. I had wanted to take care of her and ensure she had all her needs met and every comfort catered for. But seeing her sit there, at the head of the table as if on a throne, her expression loaded with reproach and disapproval, the empathy left me. Suddenly I was fine with staying where I was, standing a few chairs away from her.

Patrick brought her a cup of tea and received no thanks or even a sign of acknowledgment for it. Ellis sat to her right, his hands hovering next to hers on the table but not quite touching.

"Are you better, Mum?" I asked.

Her eyes shot in my direction. "I was shoved in a car and left to rot for a week," she spat out.

I gave her a look. "What you went through is absolutely unacceptable and I can't even begin to imagine how hard it must have been, but I talked to you on the phone three days ago, before you left home to come here."

"Well it felt like *weeks*," she replied, looking away.

"What happened?" Ellis asked carefully.

"I'm not quite sure," Mum said, and her voice quavered ever so slightly. "I came into the house, put my bags down, went to the kitchen, started tidying, and then someone pressed a cloth against my mouth. I woke up in the car, on the back bench, unable to see anything or move any of my limbs."

"Who was it?" Ellis asked.

The anger returned to her eyes. "One of *you*," she said, glaring at the whole room. Her forefinger tensed on the table, as if she wanted to point but couldn't summon the strength. "I am sure of it."

"Why?" Ellis asked as calmly as if asking about an errand.

"Who else would know about this house, or when I'd arrive, or hate me to the point of doing this to me?"

"Was it a man?" Patrick asked.

She marked a pause. "I don't know."

Patrick and I exchanged a glance, and Mum noticed. "I don't!" she insisted. "I couldn't see anything and he or she never talked. Any instruction came from some type of magnetophone, or maybe a phone, with a voice modifier."

"You didn't hear a grunt," Patrick said, "or maybe feel if it was a man or woman's hand?"

She shook her head. "They brought the food straight to my mouth and that's all the contact I had with them. Wouldn't answer me when I spoke. They didn't even carry me outside to take a piss, for heaven's sake."

"Anything at all which could point to their identity?" Ellis tried one last time.

She gazed blankly at the table in front of her. "The gloves smelled of petrol, and they always closed the door softly. I assume it's a man. It would be quite the challenge for a woman to carry me from the house to the car when I was unconscious."

"Don't underestimate women," said Charlie. "Besides, you don't know, they could've used a wheelbarrow to move you."

"Always have something clever to say, don't you?" Mum said, twisting her mouth as if biting into a lemon.

"Calm down, Mum," I said. "And Charlie has a point."

"Yes, perhaps it was *her*," she said, "or her godless woman."

"Enough," I said, wishing I didn't have to be the one defending her instead of Charlie's own mother. "I know you're still in shock, but there's no need for this. Leave Charlie and Kacey alone."

I glanced at Violette, standing in the darkness in the corner of the room. Why couldn't she and Ellis accept Charlie for who she was? It infuriated me, but I had to put this aside for now.

"I think we should go over where each one of us was, and what we did, over the last few days," Ellis said. "It's become clear there is a traitor, a murderer, amongst us, and we must rat him or her out. We will hear what everyone was doing on the twenty-second. I'll start."

He brought a fist to his mouth to clear his throat, and paused there longer than expected. "I was off work and spent the day at home. I fixed a shelf in the pantry, then did the accounts for my snooker club. I was in the study most of the afternoon, which is when Mother was taken."

"Where was Violette?" Patrick asked, leaning on the back of a dining chair.

"She had a family emergency and left on the twentieth. She returned on the twenty-third."

"Was he there when you came home?" Patrick asked Violette.

"Yes," she replied.

"And where did you go, then?"

"Carlisle, to tend to my sister," Violette replied, and stepped closer to the table so that everyone could see her. "She learned that her husband is terminally ill and needed the support, especially as I'm not spending Christmas with her this year."

"Anyone can vouch for you?" Patrick asked Ellis.

"What do you mean *vouch*?" Ellis said.

Patrick let go of the chair and turned his palms up. "We're checking alibis, aren't we? So who can confirm you were home all day, and not driving here and back?"

Ellis' face flushed. "You're insinuating *I* could have done this to Mother, and Killian?"

"Are *you* insinuating any of us is beyond suspicion?" Patrick said, shrugging.

Ellis pursed his lips and shot his brother a murderous glare.

"Don't be stupid, Patrick," Mum said. "I would have known if it had been Ellis."

"How?"

"He's my son!"

"Right, so you can rule me out too, can't you?"

She remained silent and looked away. Patrick gave a bitter laugh.

"Rule yourself out then," I said. I wanted him to prove to everyone, and Mum most of all, that it couldn't have been him.

"With pleasure," Patrick said, still staring at Mum. "I didn't take time off work until yesterday, so I was at work all day on the twenty-second."

"If I could have driven here and back in a day, then so could you," said Ellis.

"You can ask my PA, she'll tell you."

"Well we can't, can we?" I said, feeling dejected. "Not until we go back to civilisation."

"That's convenient," said Ellis.

It was Patrick's turn to glare.

"Before anyone asks," said Tilly, "I spent most of the day

Christmas shopping with my best friend, and of course we can't ask her to confirm."

"Which means I was home by myself," Lottie said. "I can see where this is going."

Ellis' gaze fell on me.

"Julian was away for work," I said, "and I spent the day helping with the Christmas preparations at the care home I volunteer for." All eyes fixed on me, and I could now feel the indignation Ellis and Patrick had both felt when it had been implied they could be the murderer. I wanted to protest and expose how outrageous the suggestion was, but I refrained from doing so, knowing how it had looked on Ellis.

"I flew on the twenty-first to Brighton for a medical convention," Julian said. "I returned home on the twenty-third." His face lit up. "I think I have proof in my coat pocket."

He got up and left the room for a moment, then returned with a piece of paper in his hand. "A receipt for my lunch," he said, going over to Ellis and Mum, "dated twenty-two December twenty nineteen." Ellis took a good look but Mum merely gazed over it before nodding – she didn't have her glasses.

Julian recovered his seat next to me.

"Charlie?" Ellis asked.

"You didn't happen to attend a rave in Scotland, over in Ullapool perhaps, purely by luck, did you?" Mum asked.

"Very funny, Granny," she said. "At work all day, and as opposed to Dad and Patrick, Bristol is a bit too far to drive here and back in a day, and I think Kacey would have noticed if I hadn't returned home."

"Kacey?" asked Ellis.

"What," she grumbled, looking like she'd much rather be in a pit of snakes than in this house, "did she come back home, or where I was on the twenty-second?"

"Both."

"Well she did come back home at the usual time, and I was working from home."

"Of course," Mum said, looking at her own liver spotted hands, "they would say this if this is both their doing. Backing each other up."

"I just–" Kacey started, then turned to Charlie and shook her head. "I just can't." And she left the room without another word.

The other answers were just as inconclusive; Leon and Melissa spent the day together at home, Leon being a primary school teacher and being off work at this time of year, and Melissa having taken time off work as a conveyancer. Patrick cynically pointed out they could have been working as a team and their alibis didn't prove a thing. Flynn was home with his father, and Rebecca and Tristan were both working in London. Tristan proved his presence in London through a time stamped photo on his phone of him in Piccadilly Circus, effectively ruling him out, which led Tilly to do the same.

"Brilliant," said Ellis. "So we've established that we could technically all be the nutter behind all this, save for perhaps three of us."

"Four," Rebecca said. "I was in London on the twenty-second. I couldn't have been here, could I?"

"There are flights to Inverness," Ellis said. "I know, I've taken them. Takes an hour and a half, and then just over an hour's drive from Inverness to the track, and another hour to the house. It would almost be quicker to do this than for me to drive here from Aberdeen."

"I was with Tristan in the morning of the twenty-second," Rebecca said.

"What about the evening?" Mum asked.

Rebecca closed her eyes in exasperation. "No. We met on the twenty-third to drive here."

"Besides," Ellis said, "if Tristan is the only one who can confirm your whereabouts, it doesn't have much weight."

"I received a card a week ago," Leon said, staring blankly in front of him. "A Christmas card. It wasn't signed, and the envelope didn't say what the return address was. It didn't wish me a happy Christmas, it just warned me not to come here this year. I ignored it, naturally. I found it curious at the time, but I forgot about it until now. Thought it was just a weird joke. But how odd is this?" He looked up at his father. "Do you think it was the madman behind all this?"

Ellis sighed. "If it was, then we know he's got a liking for you. Or she has."

"How come you've only found me now?" Mum asked the room, seemingly out of nowhere.

"What do you mean?" I asked.

"You were all here on Christmas Eve, but I wasn't. Didn't you think it odd? Did you just carry on as normal, had dinner, played a game, not a worry in the world for the old crone who birthed three of you?"

"I wanted to go and look for you," Ellis said, inching closer to her in his fervour. "I told them something wasn't right, I *told* them we had to drop everything and find out what had happened to you."

"Not that it would've done much good," Patrick scoffed. "We're stranded and without phone signal, remember?"

"But they wouldn't listen to me," Ellis went on. "They said it was nothing unexpected, that you mentioned you may be late, that you'd turn up when you turned up. I was furious."

Mum listened to all this with an impassive face, like a judge listening to claimants' sides of their stories.

"Can you blame us?" I told Ellis. "Mum warned she may not be here when we arrived, and she left a game for us to play, as if she'd planned for her absence. What else were we to think?"

Mum cocked her head at this. "A game?"

"Yes," I said, "the note you left, and the hat with the riddles."

"I did no such thing."

"Please," Charlie said, "that game could not have been written by anyone but you. No one can replicate your peculiar mind so well."

"I did not prepare a childish game for you all to play without me, you insolent child. I may be old, but I have not yet lost my mind. I know what I have and haven't done."

"Really?" Charlie said.

A wave of cold terror travelled through my blood. If that had been the murderer's doing, then this entire affair had been more premeditated than I'd thought. We were all mere puppets on a stage, playing to their rules, unknowingly doing their bidding. There was not the shade of a doubt left in my mind that the graves outside had been dug for us, and the thought of more deaths to come made me sick to my stomach.

For a few moments, I couldn't speak. And neither could anyone else. The silence settled on the dining room like shovelfuls of earth burying us and gradually blocking out all the senses.

Lottie broke the silence. "Then the books weren't from you either?"

The books! They'd flown out of my mind. "This feels like it's all a sick game for the monster behind this," I said, "and if that's the case, then I'll bet my right arm there are clues to be found in the books we received." I remembered the book I'd gotten, *Robinson Crusoe*, and the energy left me. What meaning could possibly be found there? A castaway, a remote island, cannibals, a rescue. What else was there in the story? Now I wished I'd read it.

"Can anyone translate the book they got into some kind of clue as to who the monster is, or anything about what we're going through?" I asked.

"I know *Les Misérables* well," Violette said, coming to stand next to Ellis' chair, "but I don't see what could be deduced from it. Though I noticed it was secondhand, perhaps there are notes in it?"

"You go and get it," I said. "Let's all go and get the book that was meant to be from Mum."

"I don't need to," Charlie said. "It was a new copy of *The Great Gatsby*, and I still can't believe it wasn't Granny who gave it to me, but it still makes complete sense. A party animal who seeks every physical pleasure there is, and who ends up murdered in a misunderstanding. Seems to paint me as everyone in this family sees me, and I have no doubt the lunatic is promising my death by murder."

I placed a hand on her shoulder. "Not everyone in the family, and I'll look after you."

Charlie gave me a sympathetic nod, and I left the room.

WHEN I RETURNED, Charlie was looking through the window at the other end of the room, as far away as she could from Mum, still sitting at the table. The awkwardness was thick in the air.

Kacey returned as well with her book. We all took a seat around the long dining table, save for Charlie and Lottie who remained standing.

"I brought Dad's book too," Flynn said, "just in case."

"Good idea," I said. "What was it, again?"

Flynn held the book up for everyone to see.

"A Storm of Swords," Ellis read slowly. "Never read it. Who has?"

"I've read the series," Leon said, "but I can't remember what happened in that book specifically. Give it to me, it might jog my memory."

"You've read it," I told Julian.

"I have, but same as Leon, not sure which one it is."

"Oh," Leon said as he leafed through the book. "Well, that's curious." He held the open book up in front of him. A square hole had been cut into all of the pages, about two inches wide. Leon flipped it back to have a better look. "The hole peeps onto...the first page of a chapter. And it's... Oh. *Oh.*" He looked up, and his eyes met Julian's. "Sansa's chapter. The royal wedding."

I looked from Leon to Julian, expecting an explanation, but Julian merely stared at Leon with a look of terror on his face. "What?" I pressed. "What is it?"

Leon clasped the book shut in a loud *thump*. "The erm..." Leon started. "The groom, I mean the king... He–"

"He chokes to death," Julian finished for him. "Poisoned."

"And Killian–" Tilly said, then stopped herself, bringing a hand to her mouth.

A paralysing wave of fear turned my muscles to stone. I was afraid to look at the other books, petrified to have a glimpse of what was to come. What had Julian received? I couldn't remember, and I indulged in that moment of forgetfulness.

"Oh God," Violette said, looking down at the open book on her lap. "Some entire pages are highlighted." She flipped through the book, and I caught flashes of yellow every now and then. "It's all the chapters with the Thénardiers," she said at last. "What does it mean?"

"They're pretty dodgy people, aren't they?" Patrick said. "I imagine the killer doesn't have a high opinion of you. Or Ellis."

"You think it's referring to Mum and Dad as the Thénardier couple?" Charlie asked.

Patrick shrugged. "Who knows? I got Warleggan, has anyone read Poldark by any chance?"

"I have," Julian said, "but again, it was a long time ago. I can't remember what happens specifically in that book. And I'm not sure I want to leaf through it."

"Go on," Patrick said, "we've got to know. It's a matter of survival, it may be the only way to protect ourselves, if we have an inkling of what's coming."

Julian took the novel from Patrick, leafed through it, but simply curved his mouth downwards. "No writing or holes in this one. As for the story, from what I can remember, Ross and Demelza's marriage struggles, George marries Elizabeth, romantic stuff happens with Dwight and Caroline."

"I remember that in the TV series," I said. "Was there a death?"

"Hmm, can't remember if it's in this book or the previous one, but yes Ross' cousin dies around that time."

"Yes," I say, remembering, "I think he drowned in a mine."

"Seems hardly possible here," Ellis said.

"There is a well," Lottie pointed out.

"Yes, but dry," Ellis replied.

"It doesn't have to all make sense now," Patrick said. "We just need to keep this in mind, and it may make sense later." He looked at Lottie's book in her hands, then back to his wife, anguish plastered across his face.

I couldn't see the book from her position. "Which one do you have?" I asked.

Lottie lifted the novel for everyone to see. Only one word in large glossy letters running across the cover: Poisoned. Tilly wrapped her arms around her mum's shoulders.

None of the other books were as obviously threatening as Lottie's. Rebecca's was a book titled *Pawns in the Game,* Flynn's *The Little Cockalorum,* Tilly's *Innocent Bystander,* Leon's *A Christmas Carol,* all with potential meanings but unclear without further information.

I took my courage into both hands and turned to Julian. "What did you get?" I couldn't look into his eyes – it wasn't like me.

"Crime and Punishment, remember?"

"What crime have you committed that's eating you from the inside?" Ellis asked. It was hard to tell whether he was just testing or accusing him.

Julian didn't reply straight away, then he grinned and said, "Too many to count." He winked, but no one smiled. Feel the room, and the mood, I wanted to tell him. For a fraction of a second, before he spoke, I saw a hint of a Julian I didn't know, a deep kind of sadness, or perhaps remorse, behind his plain brown eyes and glasses.

"What about you?" Julian returned. "Dante's *Inferno,* eh? What sins are you ready to renounce to begin the journey nearer to God? Is this your journey through hell?" He gestured all around. "And will the end of it terminate your spiritual rescue?"

"Or perhaps the murderer means there is no place in hell for Ellis," Patrick said.

I almost gasped. It wasn't surprising for Patrick to think this, but for him to say it out loud? I expected it from Ellis and Mum, perhaps even Violette, but Patrick had always been reluctant to join in the open enmity.

Ellis' eyes darkened, and he lifted one finger. "Listen to the rain," he said in an oddly calm tone. The wind was hurling the fat raindrops straight against the dining room's flimsy window panes. "It's filling up the well."

He didn't add anything else.

"Hey hey hey," I said. "You're playing straight into the madman's hands."

"I received a book too," Mum said, as if her own sons hadn't just threatened each other with death in front of her. "One I wasn't expecting, that is. It was on the kitchen table when I first got here, with my name on the wrapping paper. That's what I was doing when I was assaulted. Never heard of it: A Mother's Sin by Ginny Lovewell."

"They turned it into a film," Melissa said in a small voice when nobody seemed to recognise it. "I didn't read the book, only saw the film."

"What is it about?" Leon asked, and he moved to place his hand over Melissa's, but I noticed how she shifted hers away.

"A man is wanted for being a terrorist," Melissa said, looking at no one in particular, "was one of the masterminds behind a large explosion, caused many deaths, and his mother goes to great lengths to protect him. She lies, steals and breaks into places to frame other people, all to protect her son."

"How does it end?" Rebecca asked.

"The mother is arrested and gets a life sentence," Melissa replied.

"And what happens to the son?"

Melissa marked a pause. "I'm not quite sure. It's been a while since I watched it."

"He's caught too," Julian said, "and gets three hundred years in prison or something like that, you know how they are in America."

I turned to Julian. "Oh, you've read this book too?"

"No, I saw the film. *We* watched it together, don't you remember?" A hint of annoyance in his voice. "It was a long time ago, but when Melissa was talking it all came back to me. I think it was during our New York trip, when it was raining a lot and freezing cold and we ended up spending most of our time in the hotel?"

I did remember the trip, I'd been bored to death, and I think I must have been asleep when the film was playing.

"I'm starting to have an idea of who this lunatic might be," Ellis said, and everyone knew exactly who he had in mind.

A mother knowing about her son's crime, and doing everything in her power to proclaim his innocence, even breaking the law? The contradictions in the statements, the lies Patrick and Lottie knew had been told to the detectives. *I* knew it too, and to this day I couldn't fathom why they concealed the truth.

Whether this meant Ellis was guilty, no one knew – there was no conclusive forensics evidence – but the case remained unsolved to this day.

And the killer was still out there.

Nobody voiced it, but I'm sure it crossed all our minds: was Timothy's murderer the person behind all this?

Mum fixed her gaze on Patrick, and I recoiled at the venom held in her eyes. "Is this your idea of revenge?"

Patrick held her stare. If he was affected by her tone and expression, he didn't show it. "Is this an admission?" he returned.

Ellis slammed his fist on the table and I jumped out of my skin. The mugs and plates made a right clatter of noises. I was glad there weren't any knives in sight.

"Are you the *sick fuck* responsible for this?" Ellis demanded.

"No," Patrick's voice boomed, then he marked a pause to recover his cool. "No, Ellis, I am not, you utter fool. Haven't you noticed yet that I do not lower myself to your level of low blows and despicable behaviour? I will never give up on obtaining justice for my boy, but I will always stay within the law. As much as you and Mum would love to pin this on me, I do not find pleasure in inflicting pain and terror on my own family. Or anyone else for that matter."

"Who else would choose to give Great-Aunt Norah this book?" Rebecca asked. I silently begged her not to stir up more trouble; she'd already done more than enough in the past.

"I don't know," Patrick said loudly. "Anyone who's got enough sense in them to see the situation for what it is, I'd say."

"Sense?" Ellis repeated. "So the murderer is sensible, now?"

Patrick closed his eyes and took a deep breath, but it was Lottie who spoke. "That is not what Patrick meant and you know it. Listening to Melissa's summary of this story was just as hard for Patrick, for us, as it was for you. I can assure you this is not Patrick's doing, nor mine, which means that the real murderer is looking to sow trouble, and we are giving them exactly what they want. We are fighting for our survival here, and we are not going to come out of this alive if we can't keep our cool. We must work together to get out of here."

I couldn't have said it better myself, and her words helped restore some peace in the room.

"Right, nothing else we can do until the morning," I said. I felt it was better to put an end to the night now, before tensions escalated further. "Tomorrow we will look for spots with phone signal, maybe look for a bicycle too?"

"And search the house and everywhere else for someone else," Julian said. "As Patrick suggested."

I welcomed the idea that it might not be one of us.

"Yes," Ellis said, "then tomorrow we also need to look for a car that doesn't belong to us." The room erupted in noise as the chairs were pushed and everyone stood up. "If your bedroom door has a latch, use it," he added. "If not, try and block your door in any way you can, with a chair or a table. We don't know what the killer will be up to in the night."

We all climbed up the stairs in solemn silence, like a procession of monks in the middle of the night. I, for one, was only too conscious the monster could hear or see me. Perhaps they were waiting upstairs, in the loft, or in the abandoned master bedroom.

I did not want to go back to our bedroom on the second floor, and debated leaving Julian there to sleep in Killian's single bed on the first floor, but I decided against it; not only would it be insensitive, but Rebecca was on the second floor as well, and may well choose to occupy her father's room instead.

Julian held my shoulders as we entered our cold room, the curtains shivering because of the draughty window, but I was petrified and chilled to the bone. No amount of affection or heat could warm me tonight.

12

PATRICK

Nineteen years ago

Patrick could hardly understand what Lottie was trying to say on the phone amid all the sobbing. Then she calmed down long enough to say that Timothy was missing.

He didn't wait a second longer; he told her to call the police, hung up the phone, rushed out of his office, and drove home. Lottie fell into his arms.

She'd had time to gather herself, and explained. She picked him up from school, and he wanted to play with his toys outside, so she left him there and went in to put his lunch box away and fetch the laundry. She was gone ten minutes at most, but when she came back out, he was gone.

"Are you okay if I leave you alone?"

"Where are you going?" she asked.

"To look for him. But you stay here, in case he comes back."

He jumped into the car and drove around the neighbourhood. Their house was the only one on this stretch of road, with the only neighbours a good two hundred yards away. That had been a strong point in choosing to buy the house, but now he hated it. Closer neighbours may have seen something, or deterred anyone from attempting anything of this kind.

He was surprised at his own composure; he could feel the panic lurking on the outside of his mind, the catastrophe waiting to happen, but he didn't allow his thoughts to go there. His focus was heightened like never before. After a quick look up all the neighbouring streets and a word with some neighbours to keep an eye out, he saw there was no point in staying there.

He needed help, men on the ground, looking and asking around. He drove to Ellis' house. His brother's car was parked on the driveway, but when he rang the bell no one came to the door. He rang again, in rapid succession, then banged on the door, but still nothing. He peeked through the windows, walked around the house to try and have a better look, but it seemed no one was home.

He gave up and drove to his cousin's. Killian came to the door wearing a sweat suit, and frowned when he saw who it was. The smell of cigarette smoke and musty curtains wafted out of the doorway.

"Timothy's gone missing," Patrick said. "Have you heard from anyone?"

Killian's frown grew deeper. "What do you mean he's gone missing?"

"He's missing, Killian, nowhere to be seen. He was playing outside our house, and then he wasn't there anymore. Lottie heard a car leaving."

"Why would I have heard from anyone?"

Patrick sighed. "I don't know, so you haven't?"

Killian shook his head. Patrick saw young Rebecca come down the stairs behind him.

"Do you know where Ellis and Violette are? They aren't home."

Killian shook his head. "Have you told the police?"

"Yes."

"Then why don't you let them do their job?"

Patrick ignored this. "Do you know if Mum and Dad are home?" He hadn't talked to them for weeks.

"They're at my dad's today. Keeping him company, helping to look after him."

"Do you mind if I call them?"

"At dad's? That won't help much, will it?"

"No, I want to see if they stayed home for some reason."

Killian shrugged and let him in. Patrick dialled their number, and as expected, no one picked up.

"If you hear anything, let me know," Patrick said as he left.

The sense of calamity was inching closer and closer, exerting strong pressure on his mind, but he resisted it.

He had to.

13

PATRICK

Lottie is already up when I wake. She's sat on the window sill with her knees in her arms, staring outside, her eyes flitting from one detail to another. I can only see the sky from where I am, a thick layer of varying shades of grey. It looks like it has started snowing, the flakes swirling round and round. The wind is still whistling through the house. Lottie is observing the landscape as intently as if watching a film. Is she hoping to catch someone unawares?

I sit up in bed and she glances towards me, nods imperceptibly, then returns her gaze to the window. I miss the old Lottie, the one before our son's murder. Full of life, always smiling, an unwavering positive outlook on life. My opposite.

Timothy's death wasn't the turning point. I'd noticed a change before his birth. She'd become more thoughtful, she'd stopped dancing randomly in the kitchen, and our sex life had started to suffer. Life with a young child had altered our relationship further, and the loss of Timothy had been the final blow. From then on I'd lost my wife. My life too. We were both broken. Tilly gave us a reason to keep living, or I'm positive one of us – or perhaps both – would have taken our lives at some point. Not only was the loss of a son too hard to bear, but suspecting your own family of having a hand in it?

"Have you gone down yet?" I ask.

She shakes her head.

I hear voices downstairs, and suddenly have a feeling something's happened in the night. Another death? A disappearance? Tilly! I rush out of bed and don't bother changing out of my pyjamas. Last night we tried convincing her to sleep with us but she wouldn't have it.

I storm into Tilly's room and there she is, still in bed, one hand holding her phone and the other behind her head. She looks at me as if I've gone mad. I breathe a sigh of relief.

"Alright?" she says.

I go up to her and drop a kiss on her hair. "Sleep well?"

She shrugs, and that's enough for me. I go back to our room and get dressed.

When we arrive in the dining room for breakfast, I notice *something* must have happened, for the voices are agitated. Ellis is raising his voice, Charlie is shaking her head, Julian is trying to calm things. Alicia looks like she's been out all night partying, dark blue bags under bloodshot eyes.

"What's going on?" I ask.

Julian points to the table in an exasperated manner. I only see a sheet of paper, and return my gaze to Julian, confused. Then I scan the room. "Where's Mum?"

"In bed," Ellis says, "she's not well. I think she needs some rest, after everything she's been through."

"This is what's going on," Alicia says, handing me the piece of paper Julian pointed to.

It reads:

Below are two riddles.
One will tell you where you can find a gun, the other a full can of petrol.
If you find the gun first, you won't be able to use the petrol.
If you find the can of petrol first, the gun will be useless.

. . .

I turn to my siblings before I read the rest. "Is this some kind of joke?"

"You tell me," says Ellis. "But joke or not, there appears to be a can of petrol somewhere, and that is our ticket out of here. I don't know why they're doing this, whether it's a mistake, but we are going to pounce on it and use it."

"It can't be that simple," I say. "It wouldn't make sense. They won't poison Killian and hold Mum captive only to then give us the means to escape."

"Perhaps they've had a change of heart?" Alicia says.

"What about the gun and the riddles, though?" Leon says. "If they'd changed their minds, they would simply have given us the can of petrol, or told us exactly where it is. They're still planning something, and this is part of it."

"Who cares about the gun?" Charlie says. "If we all go for the can of petrol and find it, then no one will be able to use the gun, if we're to believe what's written, and we'll be able to get help."

"You don't understand," Rebecca says, coming back from the kitchen with a pot of tea she puts on the dining table. "This is all part of their plan. There is no way the murderer is giving us a way out. They'll expect us to go for the can of petrol, and then we'll fall straight into their trap."

"So what do you suggest?" Charlie asks. "We just ignore this sheet of paper, and the fact that there *is* a way to leave?"

Rebecca doesn't reply. She distributes the mugs around the table in silence.

Alicia gasps. "You're going for the gun."

Rebecca shrugs. "The murderer is one of us, so when we find out who it is, I want to be armed, both to defend myself and to take them down."

I catch Tristan from the corner of my eye. He turns to Rebecca and stares at her, as if he's not sure he heard correctly.

"Don't be silly," Flynn tells his sister. "A gun can only lead to more violence. We're trying to escape here, aren't we?"

"*You* may be," Rebecca replies, "I want to avenge Dad. That's what family does. Do you not care that Dad was murdered only yesterday?" Her voice wavers slightly.

"Rebecca…" says Ellis, slowly shaking his head. "*That* is exactly what the murderer wants. To divide us, and turn this into a game. Let's trap them in their own game, and act in unison to defeat them. We can't go wrong; if we find the petrol, we're saved."

"Yeah, because things have gone predictably so far," I say. "I hate to say it, but going for the gun makes a lot of sense." It feels odd, wrong even, to take Rebecca's side. "With a gun, we either have an advantage on the murderer, or we're on equal footing if they have one too."

"Patrick," Charlie starts, looking at me as if she doesn't recognise me, "you can't mean it."

My blood heats up. "What if every car's petrol tank is punctured? Imagine we find the can of petrol, celebrate our imminent escape, lose the gun forever, fill up a car, and one of us drives off only to run out of petrol midway along the lane. We'll have no petrol, no gun, and one laughing lunatic. And that's only one possibility, we don't know what the lunatic has planned. What if it isn't petrol in the can, what if it's water?"

"What if the gun is a fake, a toy?" Charlie replies. "The same goes if you find the gun first. We're out of a gun, and we won't have any petrol to escape."

"But we are dealing with a violent psychopath," I say. "Releasing a gun amongst us and stirring some shit sounds exactly like what they're after, so the gun is likely real. And once we have a gun, things become unpredictable. Unpredictability is our friend, and maybe our only way of escape."

A satisfying moment of silence follows. I'm acutely aware that the said psychopath is currently watching us and listening to everything, probably smiling inwardly. He or she wants us to quarrel, they must get off creating conflict. A voice tells me Mum must have a hand in this; nobody gets aroused quite as much as she does by sowing discord.

"If we have to choose between the hope of escape," Julian says, "and the certainty of more violence, blood, and pain, then I'm going for hope."

Alicia nods, and so does everyone else, save for Rebecca. I turn around to see what Lottie and Tilly think, to see if they hate me now. Tilly looks like she feels sorry for me, and I have to look away. I can stomach a lot of things, but pity from my daughter is not one of them. Lottie, on the other hand, gives me a very slight nod and steps closer to me. We exchange a look, and I think I know what's going through her mind; my family being as ruthless, treacherous, and cruel as it is, it may be time at last to respond in kind.

We are done taking hits and presenting the other cheek.

Another possibility takes form in my mind, an opportunity which would only be possible by having a gun. I can't promise that if things get heated, I won't use the threat to get answers.

I'm speechless for a short moment as I realise that subconsciously, I've been waiting all this time, coming to these stupid gatherings for years, hoping one day I might obtain the answers we owe Timothy.

"What are the riddles?" Lottie asks me.

I hand her the sheet of paper.

The gun will be found above what runs but never walks.

The location of the can of petrol is composed of two words:
The first occurs once in a blue moon, twice in Boxing Day in December, but never in May. The second is where the first lives.

I SCAN the house and its surroundings with my mind's eye, and the first thing which springs up is the tractor. It runs but never walks. I'll have to check its roof, or perhaps the barn's rafters if it's inside, but I have a feeling that's not it. It doesn't click as the obvious answer.

I glance at Lottie; she's rereading the riddles, and doesn't seem to have any idea so far. Conversation has resumed around us, everyone trying to figure out what the second riddle means. Rebecca and Tristan are whispering to each other, and I catch her eye as she peers at me sideways before returning her attention to her boyfriend.

That's the difference; those looking for the can of petrol can work together and cooperate. The gun is an individual search, unless we know for sure the other person is innocent, which is the case for me with Lottie. There is not a chance in hell I will help Rebecca.

Alicia takes the sheet of paper from me and reads the second riddle out loud for everyone's benefit. I take this moment where I don't need to be part of the conversation to observe everyone here. In all likelihood, the nutter is here, in this very room. They're all here, save for Mum upstairs, and I very much doubt she's staged her own kidnapping. Logically speaking, if I look hard enough I should be able to spot a detail, a slip, which will betray the murderer. Something which is out of character, a sign of nervousness. However diabolical their mind is, they must be nervous. The pressure will surely get to them at some point. They're risking a lot in order to... To what? Exact revenge? Settle scores? Which scores and what is there to avenge? I understand Ellis' suspicions; Lottie and I have the most at stake in terrorising them.

We have an asset. We know every single person here very well – except Tristan – so any unusual move should jump out. I just have to be watching when it happens. Ellis is being Ellis; leading the conversation, pointing to those he wants to hear from, like the conductor in an orchestra. Violette is quietly listening from the edge of the room, leaning against the door frame. She's holding a mug of coffee with both hands against her chest and has not said a single word since we've come down. Nothing unusual there.

Charlie is loud and talkative, acting as her father's counterbalance. I admire her; despite the shit she gets from most of them, she's never reacted by shutting herself down. She knows who she is and she's unapologetic. She makes herself heard no matter what people think – and these happen to be the most important people in her life. It's no small thing – I should know.

Kacey is the only one sitting down at the table. She's stirring something in her cup of tea, apparently oblivious to the heated conversation. I've known her for several years now, but I don't really *know* her. At first, when Charlie introduced her to the family, she was funny and chatty, but that quickly changed. Mum's antiquated views on what a couple should look like wore her down, and her in-laws' indifference only added to the burden. I'm surprised she's still coming to these family gatherings, but though she's physically present, she's not *with* us. I have no doubt that if there was signal or wifi, she'd be on her phone the entire time.

Tristan has walked away from Rebecca and is joining in the conversation to figure out where the can of petrol is. Other than he doesn't seem to have showered since arriving, he's acting the same way he has been since meeting him on Christmas Eve. His relationship with Rebecca is relatively new, from what I gather; I don't see how it can survive this trip. They seem like entirely different people – which can sometimes work, like Lottie and myself – but they're not compatible opposites, they're just…incompatible, I suppose. She needs someone as wicked as herself, a man to the image of her father, and Tristan seems too decent for that. She's retreated from the group with a cup of tea, and is now sulking in the corner of the room – or trying to make sense of the riddle, rather.

Flynn is very vocal about where he thinks the can of petrol is. Ellis keeps shooting his suggestions down and I can see he's getting frustrated, like a toddler about to explode into a full-on tantrum. Nothing unusual here.

Leon is standing with a cup of tea and saucer in his hand, straight as a broom. He's not really part of the conversation, but he's positioned himself so he's definitely part of the group. He's always been the quiet type, so that in itself isn't unusual, but he keeps glancing over to Lottie and me. Like me, he seems more interested in the room than solving the riddle. Even Melissa, who's quieter than him, has her gaze fixed on whoever's talking, following closely what's being said. She may not talk much, but I'm convinced she has a better idea of where that can of petrol is than anyone else. She strikes me as the type to be easily underestimated just because she's small and unassuming, even by her husband; Leon doesn't appreciate her nearly as much as he should, in my opinion. But does that mean she's morally capable of pulling this off? If she is, she's a bloody genius at concealing it. She's never voiced any displeasure towards the family. She looks like she couldn't bring herself to step on a spider, but that may just be why she's a good candidate.

Lottie asks what are my thoughts on the riddle, so I have to put an end to my careful observation. Tilly has left us and joined the other group.

"I think the riddle's too vague," I reply in a low voice. "There are too many potential locations. The tractor, the barn, the bridge—"

"The bridge?" Lottie interrupts.

"The river runs but never walks, and the bridge is above it."

"We'll never have enough time to check every location carefully."

"Maybe that's the point," I say, turning away as Rebecca looks over. I don't know if she can lip read. "Their riddle seems harder to solve, but the gun is harder to find even once the riddle is solved."

"Should we separate to look in different places at once?" she asks.

I nod. "Ideally. But I'd rather you not wander the property on your own."

"I can look after myself."

"None of us can look after ourselves until we know who the murderer is. They've got the element of surprise. They've got control over the situation."

"So you're not any safer than I am. Why me?"

I hadn't thought that far, and I mark a pause as the reason hits me. "Because I'm more expendable. Tilly will be better off with you."

The light in her eyes flickers. She looks like she wants to protest, but lets go. "Well," she says, "as far as we know, the house isn't any safer. Finding the gun may mean we both survive, and I'd rather be outside anyway, checking for phone signal."

I nod. I didn't expect her to settle comfortably into a chair and read a book. I glance over at the others; they've started speaking in lower tones, which may mean they're getting somewhere with the riddle. "You go and check the tractor and the barn," I tell Lottie. "The tractor runs but doesn't walk, so it could be on its roof, or anything you see that is above it. Let's meet back here after."

She nods and heads off instantly. I follow her out, but not before noticing Leon's look in his eyes. He's understood we are getting close.

I grab my coat and hastily step into my wellingtons. A frosty gust of wind meets me as I open the door. I watch Lottie trot away. I know I will never see the Lottie I fell in love with again; even though this torment is bringing us closer, a part of us died twenty years ago.

There was one year, when Timothy was still around, where my Lottie returned, and we experienced the bliss of peaceful family life. Timothy was three. We'd powered through the challenges of being first time parents with a young child. We'd signed Timothy up full time in nursery, freeing up some valuable time for ourselves. I'd received a promotion, and with the extra income we'd gone on nice family holidays, and I remember enjoying every minute. Lottie and I had recovered our excitement and lust of old, and we found mad pleasure in sneaking intimate moments anytime Timothy was out of the house or asleep. I'd finally had a taste of what it was like to be a happy father and husband. It was, by far, the happiest year of my life. Then the tragedy happened, and that feeling vanished forever.

What I wouldn't give, or do, to go back to that year.

I bury my face in the coat's collar and make my way to the river, to get it over with. Ever since Timothy, I can no longer go for walks alongside rivers. I always try to steer clear of them as much as I can. Sometimes I see a floating object, or a reflection, and I can't help but see my son's bloated corpse on the surface. Or other times a rock on the bank looks like it could be a child's body, only half submerged by the lapping water, and I know that night I will have nightmares.

A glance behind me, and I glimpse Leon in the distance just before he disappears behind a tree. It suddenly hits me; he doesn't care about the can of petrol. He only positioned himself with the others not to be openly scorned. He wants the gun too, and thinks he may be able to snatch it before me, if I lead him to it.

I slow down for a moment, trying to gather my thoughts. I had never thought him so sneaky. Kind, smiley, even meek Leon. What would he do with a gun? I can't imagine he knows what a catch is, or that he'd have the moral strength to pull the trigger on anyone. He's my nephew, I've known him his whole life. I can't be wrong about this, can I?

If he's hoping I'll lead him to the gun, then he must not have solved the riddle, and perhaps he won't understand why I'm going to the river. I don't change my course, I head straight for the bridge to make my intention as clear as possible. When I reach the log store and I know his line of sight is broken, I shuffle sideways and creep along the wall of stacked logs. I wait for him to be level with my position, and I walk in the opposite direction, back where we came from, using the tall pine trees as cover if he happens to look back.

I head straight for the abandoned circular well. I think my two best options are the bridge and the well, one above a river, the other above an underground spring. If Leon wants to join me on the bridge, then I'd rather delay that exploration till later.

I hear steps to my right. I turn around to see Leon running towards me. No, towards the well! I get sprinting too. I'm much closer so I get there before he does, but where do I look now? My heart is racing and knowing I must be quick stalls my mind. He's going to catch up in a second, and then what?

There is nothing on the ground around the well, nothing hanging down the shaft. The mossy stones which line the inside vanish into a bottomless pit of black. I lift the flagstones arranged into a circle and there, in a gap between two slabs, black metal against matt rock, lies a revolver. I grab it and a sense of relief runs through me. Leon can catch up now, it no longer matters.

"Shite," I hear him mutter several paces behind me, panting. "You're not the looney at least, are you?" he asks.

I don't reply. I've opened the cylinder and...it's not loaded. Not a single bullet in the chambers.

My blood runs cold, and my tongue is like bone dry wood. Is that what the letter meant? Have they found the can of petrol, which means now we can't use the gun? I scan the well once more, searching for any clue as to where the ammunition might be.

"Patrick?" Leon asks, still catching his breath.

A tiny little chest catches my eye, hanging where the bucket to scoop water would once have hung. The type of quaint little box that could be used as a salt cellar. I reach for it, but stop when I notice that the wire it's attached to goes around a pulley, then runs down the side of the rusty metal structure holding the pulley up, and then buries itself in the sparse grass. It strikes me as odd, but I hear Leon step closer so I hastily snatch the box down and open it. Six bullets.

The wire comes to life, leaps from the ground like an incredibly long and thin snake, and a second later, at the edge of the copse a short distance away, a loud explosion.

The ground shakes, a cloud of black smoke rises behind the barn, and I am paralysed. Leon could take the revolver and bullets from my hands right now, and I wouldn't budge.

But he doesn't.

14

ELLIS

(Ten minutes earlier)

Outwardly, I'm leading the conversation, guiding the search for the answer to the riddle. But inwardly, I'm still reeling from the fact that not everyone is looking for the fuel. Do they not see that working together to find it is the only way out of here? The more we comply with the murderer's plans, the more screwed we are. And it couldn't be clearer to me that the murderer's plan is to divide us and make us fight each other.

Did I really expect anything else from Patrick, though? He's always gone against the stream, especially if Mother and I are the stream. Always wants to stand out, to draw the attention to himself, and it doesn't matter if the attention is negative. I don't know if it's a youngest child thing, but it's certainly always been the case with him. I doubt he actually believes what he's saying about the gun. He has a sharp mind, I'll give him that, and I'm certain he could come up with convincing arguments to defend any position on Earth, but did he decide to go for the gun simply because I made it clear I was going for the can of fuel?

I barely slept last night – I doubt anyone here did – so I tried putting myself in the killer's shoes. I'm afraid the person who fits the bill best is Patrick. The killer obviously holds a grudge against the Morrisons, and wants to make us pay for a past offence. The book he gave Mother couldn't be more self-explanatory. So far only two people have been openly targeted: Killian, who was a suspect in Timothy's death and who has never gotten along with Patrick, and Mother, whom Patrick thinks is hiding something. Coincidence?

Perhaps he couldn't bring himself to killing his own mother, so he only took her away to terrorise her. I have no doubt I'm next, and he won't have those qualms with me. All those years ago, it never came as a surprise when Patrick and Lottie barely waited twenty-four hours before pointing the finger. Just because I've always drawn attention to how, his entire life, he's spent every effort trying to prop himself up at the family's expense, then surely I *must* have murdered his only child. The logic is irrefutable.

Him going for the gun, and Lottie following him, is telling too. And you know what? I bet he'll find it first, before we find the bloody fuel. He knows where he hid it, after all.

"I'm sorry but this riddle doesn't make any sense," says Charlie. "The murderer's done it on purpose because they don't want us to find the petrol."

"That's unhelpful, Charlie," I say. "I think Alicia has a point; we're fixating on the wrong things. It doesn't matter exactly how often a blue moon appears, it was probably meant allegorically."

"Twice in December," says Flynn, "it must be 'holiday', right? There are two bank holidays: Christmas and Boxing Day."

"Twice on *Boxing Day* in December, it says," I point out, annoyed at the time we're wasting by going nowhere. "And never in May, it goes on to say. There is always a bank holiday in May."

"Then snow?" Flynn returns. "It's not impossible to get two snow showers on Boxing Day, but it never snows in May, and you could say it snows once in a blue moon."

I can't help but roll my eyes.

"Good thinking," Alicia says, "but snowing twice on Boxing Day, that can't be right. And even if we accepted snow to be the first half of the answer, then it reads, *The second is where the first lives*. Where does snow live?"

"The sky?" Flynn guesses. "The ground? The clouds?"

"So we'll find the can of petrol in the clouds?" I scoff. "You go and look for it there, Flynn, be my guest."

I know he must be shooting daggers at me, so I don't meet his eyes. Why won't he just shut up? He's slowing us down.

"What if we list everything we usually do on Boxing Day?" Julian says. "Not us, but people in general. The traditions. And then we can see if anything happens twice, and go from there."

That'll take ages, and Patrick and Lottie are whispering to each other now, but I don't have a better idea so I don't object.

"We eat the leftovers from Christmas Day," Alicia says. "Mince pies, sausage rolls, maybe bake a quiche."

"And cheese," Julian adds. "Lots of cheese and crackers."

"Games," Charlie says, and I notice she refrains from listing the games, because otherwise she'll have to say charades and none of us wants to think of that again.

"A lot of people go for swims in ice cold water," I say. "Or eccentric runs."

"Charity events," Melissa says. I almost jump at her voice; I hadn't noticed she was next to me.

"Shopping," says Tilly. "Isn't it one of the busiest days of the year for the high street shops?"

I'm getting impatient, and it's clouding my judgement. I can't get my brain to analyse the riddle and find possible routes. And now Patrick and Lottie are leaving the dining room and heading for the front door. They're too quick, dammit.

"People give money to those who serve," Tristan says. "It's an old tradition, but some people still do it."

"There are enough of you working on this," Leon says as he puts his cup of tea down on the table. "I'll go and look for a bicycle outside, and search the grounds for an intruder while I'm there."

I nod. Not like he was contributing anyway.

"On the paper," Kacey says out of nowhere, and all heads turn in her direction. "Does it say *on* Boxing day, or *in* Boxing Day? I was sure I heard *in* when you read it, Alicia, but everyone acts as if if it said *on* Boxing Day."

Alicia straightens the sheet of paper in front of her and reads out loud. "The first occurs once in a blue moon, twice *in* Boxing Day in December, but never in May."

Kacey nods. "I don't think it's a typo. And if it was meant on purpose, then the meaning of the words is irrelevant. It's about the letters, and I've narrowed it down to two options: n, and b. *N* doesn't mean anything on its own, but *b* is a word."

"Bee," I repeat.

"Hive!" Alicia shouts. "A bee lives in a hive."

"You're a genius," I tell Kacey. I've never warmed to her in all the years I've known her, but right now I could kiss her. "Yes, the beehive, Mother set one up a while ago!"

Kacey gets up from her chair.

"I'll go," Flynn says immediately.

Kacey freezes mid-air. She's a triathlete and in great shape, and she's the one who solved the riddle, so I'm happy for her to go and retrieve the can of fuel, but I don't want to tell Flynn off once again.

"How about you both go," Alicia suggests. "It's safer anyway."

They race out. I think we can see the edge of the copse from the dining room window, so I walk over. We may even be able to see the beehive itself.

Charlie comes to stand next to me. She's uncharacteristically close; I hesitate to glance her way. I can smell her perfume, a faint whiff of Channel Mademoiselle.

"I'm proud of you, Dad," she says.

Well, that's awkward. I catch a glimpse of her in the glass' reflection, and she's also struggling to look my way.

"What for?"

"For looking for the can of petrol. Doing the right thing."

I turn around, and catch Alicia's look. She gives me an encouraging smile; can't remember the last time she did that. Did they really think me so heartless and selfish as to turn against my own family? I know they mean well, but I take it as an insult. Why are they surprised that I want to get us out of here?

"Right," is all I can bring myself to say. I'm too stunned to voice my confusion. If I say anything else, it will start an argument and right now I just want Flynn and Kacey to return with the can of fuel.

They appear outside, Flynn running slightly ahead of Kacey. In this case, the competition is good. They're pushing each other, and the quicker they get to the fuel, the sooner the gun will be rid of, and the quicker we can get out of here.

"Kacey impressed me," I say, venturing on safer grounds. "You chose a bright one."

She raises an eyebrow at me, understandably. It may be the first time I pay her wife a compliment.

"Maybe I haven't...appreciated her as much as I should have, in the past," I add.

She gives me a look I can't quite make out. Sadness? Regret? Emotion?

She opens her mouth to say something, but a thundering explosion makes the window panes shake, and a large cloud of black smoke appears where the beehive should be.

I can no longer see Kacey or Flynn.

We rush out.

15

REBECCA

Above what runs but never walks. It should be easy, but I can't focus and think properly.

I hate everything about this situation. Why are we all playing this madman's game? He killed my father, for Christ's sake. We'd be tying up every man here and torturing them until they talked, if I had my way. At first his death numbed me; I felt nothing and transitioned into a trance-like state. People were talking around me, moving, crying, but it was like I was watching from the outside. Or on a screen, and I was on my sofa at home.

Then the crying started, as I thought of the good moments I shared with Dad. He wasn't a perfect father, or even a good one by any standard, but he was mine, and I loved him. It was the suddenness of it which shocked me. He still had so many years ahead of him, and then in a minute or two, he was gone. In front of my eyes. He'd looked so vulnerable, defenceless, innocent, as he lay motionless on the threadbare rug.

Now the tears have stopped, and I want blood. The murderer is here, and I want that gun to take him down. I don't know exactly what I'll do once I have it, but I'll cross that bridge when I come to it. I can be creative when I want to. First I need to solve that ridiculous riddle, and Tristan won't help me, and I can't *think*. That just riles me further.

I can't help but look at this boyfriend of mine as he helps the others solve their riddle. I know he's right for me; he's the breath of fresh air I've needed, the guiding light which will keep me on the path to happiness. He soothes me and we work well together. I like to direct and he likes to be directed. But why isn't he helping me now? We're supposed to be a team. Together we might beat Patrick and Lottie. As it is, there's no way I'll find the bloody gun before them, and it's all on him.

Flynn and Kacey rush out of the house. They must have solved it. Good for them – and us all, I suppose. If we get out, the police will do their job and find who the murderer is. Well, I hope they will, anyway. If they're as incompetent as the ones who investigated Timothy's death, then we'll never know.

A part of me wants to be rescued – of course I do, the certainty of surviving beats anything else – but the other part doesn't. The best way to make the madman pay is to discover myself who it is and take things into my own hands. Dad always said, 'No one can serve you better than yourself,' and here he's right. I can't rely on the police to do their job correctly. They failed Patrick and Lottie, why wouldn't they fail me too?

A loud blast rings out, and at first I think Patrick's found the gun and shot someone.

Then I see the black smoke, know it can't be the gun, and it hits me.

Flynn.

I run outside, push Melissa out of the way to sprint past the front door before her. My legs are moving of their own accord; I've never run so fast in my entire life. I catch up to Ellis and run past him. I can't feel my feet, or care about my heart thumping in my chest, or the air burning in my throat.

The explosion has broken trees, some branches are alight with fire. I see someone on the grass, but I quickly recognise Kacey. She's not moving, but I keep running; Flynn was quicker than her, and therefore was closer to the petrol when it exploded.

I finally see him, crushed under a tree about half a foot wide. The acrid stench of petroleum smoke hits my senses. I feel sick, but I don't think it's the smoke's doing. I step over blackened branches and away from the ring of leftover petrol flames.

"Flynn," I call out when I reach him.

I recoil as I see his face; it's covered in blood, mixed in with black lumps and gashes across his forehead and into his hairline. The tree trunk is pinning him down across his chest. I move to roll it off him, but stop myself; it will just hurt him more. I call on all the strength I have to lift one end and make it pivot away from my brother. It's heavy though, and as I throw it sideways, thinking it will land well away from him, it falls short and flat on his foot.

He doesn't budge.

Every inch of my body freezes. Why didn't he cry out in pain?

I bend over him and turn his head. His eyes are closed, his neck limp.

"No," I shout in his face, "no no no, Flynn. Don't you dare. Open your eyes!"

I place my ear on his chest, but can't distinguish between a potential heartbeat and the steps behind me as the others reach us.

I place my hand under his nose. His lips are cold, and I can't feel any air.

I let a scream of agony escape my lips, and collapse onto the forest floor by his corpse. Alicia comes to my side, tries to lift me for an embrace, but I ignore her.

My brother, my closest friend...

I stay there for a while, oblivious to everything else.

My brain switches to autopilot as they drag me back to the house. It seems Kacey's still alive. Tristan walks by my side in silence. Thank God for that. Once in the house, I tell him I want to be alone and head up to our room.

As I succumb to the sheer force of Flynn's absence, knocking me down on the bed, I realise the anger I felt following Dad's death isn't directed solely towards the killer, or to the fact that he's dead and he shouldn't be. I'm furious at myself, because what I felt for Dad wasn't sadness, but relief.

Sadness is what I'm feeling for Flynn now. Crippling grief, the epitome of unfairness. A sense that nothing will ever be right again. A darkness that will haunt me for the rest of my life. But with Dad, no, it is relief; a pressure lifted off my shoulders. His judgement no longer weighing on me, his nagging comments gone forever. A sense of freedom, really. And how can I feel so…good?…following the death of my own father.

Something's not right with me. Yet a part of me *is* right, because I know what I'm feeling now for Flynn is exactly what I should be feeling after the unjust death of my baby brother.

And it's so powerful, so painful, that I want to forget everything.

16

LEON

The house falls quiet, but not in a peaceful way. The silence is heavy, laden with the threat of incoming darkness. Kacey is battling for her life in a room. Rebecca is mourning, and so is everyone else. Great-Aunt Norah is still recovering from her ordeal. The air is thick with pain, all the possible varieties of it, and it's suffocating. I can no longer stay inside.

The air outside is crisp and invigorating. The isolation of the place is its own blessing and curse. As I stand on the front porch, I'm grateful for the total absence of traffic noise and human presence; for a fleeting moment, I even enjoy the peace and melodious noises of nature unperturbed by the crippling anxiety of our situation. In front of me the tall pine trees sway in unison to the rhythm set by the wind, like a choir of giants. The grey clouds above move quickly towards the east, like reflections in the surface of a river, and I wish I could jump on them and surf away. The only sign of life comes from the crows, blackbirds, and swallows, and the distant rush of the river, a reassuring white noise. But of course, it's the very absence of civilisation which is the cause of all this.

I light a cigarette and breathe in the sweet poison of comfort. It brings me back home, where life may not have been perfect, but at least it was safe. Makes me re-evaluate a whole lot of things. If I make it out of here, I will take it as an opportunity to start over. To treat the people in my life better, to enjoy the small things, not to worry about petty primary school politics. How silly my colleagues seem now that I think of their complaints. Who has the time to worry about unhappy parents and sick pay? People whose lives are not immediately threatened, that's who.

The front door opens behind me and I start, unsure if it's the killer about to spring on me. But it's only Julian, the cuffs of his shirt stained with blood. He looks drained, the colour in his cheeks gone.

"How's Kacey?" I ask but instantly regret it; the last thing he wants, I imagine, is to go on about the cause of his exhaustion.

He shakes his head. "Nothing else I can do for now." He closes the door behind him and stands by the pillar opposite the one I'm leaning on.

"Let's leave all that inside, shall we?" I suggest. "I long for a normal chat."

He gives me a restrained smile. I offer him a cigarette, but he waves his hand.

"Wouldn't say no to smoking something else, though," he says, eying me sideways. "God knows I need to release the tension."

"Ah, not anymore I'm afraid. Those days are behind me. Now I just stick to the good old nicotine."

"A shame," says the surgeon. "How's everything with you? Before…"

"Good. Well, not bad. I have my eye on the deputy principal position, but it's probably a long shot."

"Oh, look at you," he says with forced sympathy. "That would be a good step forward."

I shrug. "I'd rather have a happy marriage, if I'm honest."

He looks away, as if uncomfortable. But if we're going to have a normal chat, what else can I talk about? It's not like we have a lot of things in common. And besides, I have no one to talk to about these things.

"I thought you two were doing well," Julian says.

"We're okay, I suppose. Melissa just feels more distant lately. We haven't been intimate for a long time, and it feels like she's avoiding me."

"Have you tried to bring it up with her and tell her how you feel? Communication often resolves most relationship problems."

Why does he have to take that *doctor* tone? I just want an honest chat with my uncle.

"I've tried, but she just says everything's fine and then changes the subject or leaves the room. And I know everything is not fine. Maybe this tension will get her to open up. You'd think after six years of marriage we'd be as open as a couple can be." I give a joyless chuckle.

Julian takes his glasses off and cleans the lenses with the lip of his shirt. "Do you want me to have a chat with her? It seems to me she's the one who's not communicating, and if it comes from someone else she may take it more seriously."

"No, it's fine, don't worry about it. We'll get through it, I'm sure. Don't feel like you have to do anything about this, I just wanted to share and get it off my chest. I'm not asking for your medical opinion."

"Sorry, I tend to do that. I guess it's because most people I talk to expect me to help in one way or another. And that's fair enough. It does get tiring after a while, though." His gaze drifts away.

"I can imagine," I say. "I bet you're looking forward to retirement and finally taking it easy."

A melancholy smile forms on his lips but he stays silent for a moment. "I wouldn't mind a few years of sipping on a cocktail by the beach in Portugal, I'll admit."

There's something in his voice, or on his face, that says the opposite. I sense there's something he isn't telling me, an elephant in the room.

"Any plans for retirement?" I probe in between two puffs.

He shrugs. "Too far away still."

"Oh go on," I say. "It can't be more than what, two years?"

He raises an eyebrow. "Are you saying I'm old?"

I laugh, and it feels good. "Well..." I wince in a teasing way, then laugh some more. "I'm just kidding. But I remember Alicia telling me, I think it was last Christmas, that you were thinking about early retirement. And given the stress you go through on a daily basis, it only makes sense."

"I don't know. It seems like a forbidden pleasure. I could definitely use the rest, but there are other things at play. It's not just about me." He glances at his watch, then adds, "Time to get back inside and check on Kacey."

I nod, and he leaves. I know I should go back in too, but I can't bring myself to face the stress yet.

So I stay outside a little longer.

17

PATRICK

Nineteen years ago

The wait was unbearable. His son, his only child, was in danger, and there was nothing he could do. Right at this moment, Timothy was somewhere in Scotland, probably panicked, perhaps being harmed. And the police's only advice was to stay home. How could he just stay home and *wait*?

The sun was going down, the house slowly plunging into darkness, but they didn't turn the lights on. They didn't drink, eat, or talk. What was the point? None of that would bring Timothy back. Talking would only bring their level of anxiety up a notch. Patrick had needed to urinate for a couple of hours, but he couldn't bring himself to go to the toilet and risk missing the phone ring.

He hoped with all his heart that it was all an accident, that Timothy had hidden in a bid to play hide and seek, and he'd gotten stuck somewhere. Or that he'd run away on his own for some incomprehensible reason. But as much as he wanted to believe it, he knew it to be impossible. He'd searched every inch of the garden, of the nearby woods, even the closest neighbours' gardens. It could only be an abduction, but who could possibly do this to them? Were they just victims of bad luck, a criminal randomly driving around and spotting an opportunity?

He paced around the living room and the hallway, checking the phone's connections every now and then. He looked out of the window regularly too, in case he saw something, Timothy or any other sign, or to see if perhaps the police would pay them a visit.

Then the phone rang, and Lottie pounced on it like a cat on a mouse. Patrick rushed to her side and listened to the muffled voice.

They found a corpse in the river, he heard the man say, half a dozen miles from their house, and it matched Timothy's description.

Lottie dropped the phone and it bounced up and down on the cord, like a yoyo.

Patrick's throat closed. For a few seconds, he forgot to breathe.

The police officer kept talking, but they ignored him.

The world had turned on its head.

∾

A PAIR of men showed up at the house that night to take statements. They returned the next day, in the afternoon, to update Patrick and Lottie on the investigation and to check on them.

"We don't yet have any lead for a suspect," the rotund officer with a thick brown beard said. "We have a few sightings of cars in the area around the time you called in, we'll try to find them and follow up on that. We spent the entire day taking statements. Your neighbours didn't notice anything out of the ordinary. One did mention hearing a rapid acceleration from a car on Birch Street, we assume it was the same one you reported, Mrs Morrison, but they didn't see the car itself. Your brother was at his house all day, along with his wife and your parents. He was taken ill and they came to assist. Your cousin Killian–"

"Hold on," Patrick said. "I went to Ellis' house as soon as I heard. I rang the bell and knocked several times, but nobody came to the door. Ellis' car was there, but not Violette's, and certainly not my parents'."

The officers eyed each other but didn't say a word.

"My parents were at my uncle's in Dundee," Patrick resumed, "Killian himself told me yesterday. My sister said the same on the phone; she talked to our mother the day before yesterday."

"Mr. Morrison," the bearded officer said, "your brother came down with an illness yesterday, which probably changed your parents' plans."

"No," Patrick said firmly. "No, my brother wasn't home, or if he was and was simply too ill to come down, I can assure you no one else was there. I looked inside, and stayed a good ten minutes, ringing and knocking, I would have seen or heard something. What about the missing cars? Killian told me yesterday afternoon that my parents were in Dundee, after they supposedly changed their plans."

The bearded man sighed and brought his hands together. "With respect, Mr. Morrison, if you do not have evidence of their presence in Dundee other than your word, then it has no weight for us. We will call your uncle to cover all ends, but the statements have been corroborated by all parties involved so far. No one coming to the door when you paid a visit does not mean the statements are false. They may have nipped out to get medication and supplies."

Was this really happening? His world was spinning. He wanted to grab the man by his collar and shake sense into him.

"Or perhaps they were deliberately ignoring you," the officer added. "Who knows what the family dynamics are." He gave Patrick a look then that meant, *clearly things aren't well if you're trying to frame your own brother.*

Patrick didn't think it possible, but things had just taken a turn for the worse.

18

TRISTAN

We're all huddled around Kacey's bed. She's unconscious, but at least she's breathing. She looks broken; the tree branch hit her square on the head and chest, but her entire body seems unnaturally bent. Alicia's cleaning her wounds with some cotton wool, Violette and Charlie are hugging each other, sobbing, and Ellis is staring at Kacey, as if trying to heal her through telepathy. Tilly is sobbing uncontrollably into her mother's shoulder. I had no idea she was so close to Flynn.

I'm torn; I want to be with Rebecca, to comfort and support her in any way, but she told me not to follow her. It doesn't feel right, she shouldn't grieve on her own. In the space of just twenty-four hours, she's lost her immediate family. I can't begin to imagine what that feels like, especially since she and Flynn were close.

Patrick is standing in the doorway, unsure whether to step in or not. Nobody has blamed him yet, but the accusation is thick in the air. He makes way for Julian to come back into the room with some medical supplies, but even Julian gives him the cold shoulder. And why not? Had he not gone for the gun, and found it first, Flynn would still be here, and Kacey wouldn't be fighting for her life. At least he has the decency not to parade the gun in front of us.

"I must warn you," Julian tells the room as he bends over Kacey, "I can't work miracles, so don't expect the impossible from me. I'm not going to be able to do much with a few bandages, some pure alcohol, and a granny's sowing kit." He gestures angrily at the bag he just brought in.

"Nobody expects the impossible, darling," Alicia says. "Just do your best, that's all you can do."

"She needs to be in a damn hospital," Julian adds. "This is a farce."

I've set out to keep a close eye on everyone. They're all in this room, so the next thing that happens should be noticeable; whoever's missing must be the killer. Well, Rebecca isn't here, she went back up to our room for a bit of quiet, but I'm fairly safe in the knowledge it's not her. Or Norah.

Not for the first time, I think about the chain of events which brought me here. If I'd never been to the climate march six months ago, I would never have met Rebecca. Hell, if I'd just gone home that night, instead of getting shitfaced, I would not have met her. If she hadn't defeated every one of my arguments on climate change, making me doubt the facts I had never wavered from before, I may not even have fallen for her. I'd found it fascinating how she'd managed to make the anti-climate arguments sound sensible. It didn't change my mind, but it made me fall in love with the sharpness of her brain. Her looks didn't hurt, either. But her stance on the environment should have been a bright red flag.

We've only just met each other, really. What possessed me to go to the end of the world and spend Christmas away from my family? My mother gave me the cold shoulder for weeks when I told her. They all begged me to stay for Christmas, but no. I had to go for the adventure, to flick off my family for a girl, to spend every fucking second I could with her. Like a needy puppy.

"Everyone leave the room," Julian says loudly. "It's too crowded in here, let's give her some space to breathe."

We all shift into Ellis and Violette's bedroom. Nobody wants to go downstairs, it'd feel like we're abandoning Kacey.

"I feel like we should be doing something," Ellis says. "To neutralise the killer. To take them off guard."

"What do you have in mind?" Alicia asks.

Patrick and Lottie are in the room too, away from the rest of us, tucked in the corner. They haven't said a word yet since they've come back inside with the gun. Not that I've heard, anyway.

"Maybe we should lock everyone in separate rooms," Ellis suggests. "To make sure they don't strike again."

"They didn't need to strike just now," Charlie says. "The killer might as well have been locked in a room, Flynn would still have died."

"It does seem like we're doing their job well enough for them," Ellis says, openly staring at Patrick. "But I have to disagree with you," he tells Charlie, "because if Patrick had been locked in a room, he would not have found the gun, and the explosion would not have taken place."

"The logistics don't work," Leon says. "Who locks us up? Who will the last person be, and how will they be locked up? What if that last person is the killer?"

"Tristan, Tilly, or Julian could be the last person," Ellis replies. "They've proven they can't be the killer."

Leon winces. "I don't think we should accept certainty on anything, in our situation. If someone had told me, before I got here, that one of us would be responsible for this madness, I would have bet my life against it."

"It won't work," Patrick says. "I oppose locking everyone up, and I've got the gun."

Ellis gives a high-pitched hysterical laugh. "So that means you're the murderer!"

Patrick's eyes darken. "I currently have the deadliest weapon of all tucked into my belt. I am the only one with a gun – openly, that is – so I have all the power. What is stopping me from announcing it's me and just killing you all?"

"You only have six bullets, and there are more of us," says Ellis.

A sour smile forms on Patrick's lips. "You don't think I could get creative enough to get everyone killed anyway?" He wipes the smile off his face. "No, I repeat once more, I am *not* the killer. Which means I can't trust any of you, and we are not getting locked in a room unless I'm the last one to do it, and I doubt there will be a consensus here to trust me with your lives. That's why it won't work."

I can't bring myself to believe Patrick guilty of all this. A big man like him – the biggest in this family – it would be too obvious, and beyond that, it just doesn't seem to suit his style. He's not sneaky, or underhanded, or sadistic. To my mind, he's more likely to kill everyone in a sudden fit of anger.

A chilling scream rings out from upstairs. My skin turns rock hard all over my body.

No...

Not the only person I know here?

19

NORAH

Nineteen years ago

"Why are they back?" Norah asked Killian.

"Double checking statements, they said," her nephew replied. "Apparently Patrick had some objections."

"Typical. But what do they want with Rebecca? She's only a silly little girl."

Killian shrugged.

She couldn't take her eyes off the detectives in the garden. Two imposing men in suits talking to a young impressionable girl, they could make her say anything they wanted.

"Is it even legal to question a minor without a parent present?" she asked to no one in particular.

Killian shrugged. "They weren't going to write down her statement officially," he said, "they were arguing about it, the short one wanted to, the bearded one didn't, then Rebecca mentioned seeing a child's cardigan yesterday, and something switched. That's when they took her away into the garden."

"She needs to shut her gob and leave family matters as they should be, private," Norah said. "You're her father, they can't refuse you. Make her come back."

"They already told me not to follow them out. What do you want me to do?"

"Go and tell them you're worried about the impact this questioning will have on her wellbeing."

Killian hesitated, then walked out, but Norah knew it would fail. He was too weak. As much as she liked him, he had no spine. Few did, compared to her.

The bearded man blocked Killian's path and gestured for him to return inside, which he did with his tail between his legs.

When the questioning ended, the officers thanked them for their time and left.

Rebecca could barely look at Norah and her father. She bit her lower lip and stared at her great-aunt's knees.

"What did you tell them?" Norah demanded.

"Not much," the twelve-year-old said, "just what I saw, Violette talking to Dad outside her car not long after Patrick came over, and she had a green cardigan in her hands. It looked like it could be a child's. They asked so many more questions but I didn't know the answers."

Norah massaged her temples. "You realise what you did, don't you? You've single handedly made the entire family look like criminals. What you said, you silly little girl, will affect not only you and your father, but everyone else. Did you think of the trouble Ellis will be in now? Or what Patrick and Charlotte will now think? Do you think we need the stress? You have no idea what you think you saw, and yet now the entire nation will see the Morrisons as a murdering and conniving family."

Rebecca just stood there, biting her lip, stealing occasional glances at Norah, and her mindless silence just inflamed her further.

"All because you don't know what you saw," she went on. "You've detracted the detectives from their trail, directed them to us when they could be using this time to look for the actual murderer. While they're focusing on us, the murderer is escaping, covering his trails, and getting away with it. You helped these detectives turn innocent and meaningless details into something bigger, and all for what, to gain attention? What do you have to gain by hurting your own family? Well, whatever it was, you will have attention now. Enough to last you a lifetime."

"Stupid girl," Killian added under his breath.

Norah turned to her nephew. "I will hire a solicitor. These detectives breached some form of procedure, or protocol, I am sure of it. There is no way a twelve-year-old's statement in a back garden can hold any legal weight. I will not have this family slandered." She turned to Rebecca. "And come Monday, you will have another chat with these detectives and retract everything, saying you were just looking for attention, or by God…"

20

CHARLIE

As everyone rushed upstairs, I deliberately lingered behind. I was dying to know what could possibly be happening now upstairs, but the killer *must* prepare his next move when everyone's attention was elsewhere. That was how they could set everything up without anyone noticing; distraction must be their tool of choice.

So I scanned Dad and Mum's room while everyone filed out. At first glance, nothing suspicious jumped out. When I turned to leave the room, my eyes met Melissa, still hovering in the hallway, staring at me through the doorway. I couldn't determine what kind of look it was. In the surrounding darkness, her light blue eyes acquired an ethereal quality. I'd always found her attractive, but I chased the thought out of my head; this was not the time to fantasise. We held each other's gaze for several seconds, which felt like minutes. Was she suspecting me, because I was staying behind? I couldn't detect any mistrust in her eyes, though. More like she was trying to tell me something, like she was about to open her mouth to speak, but she decided against it, turned around, and disappeared into the stairs.

I cast a look down the hallway, left and right; no moving shadows.

No movements disturbing the light behind any of the closed bedroom doors.

A wooden floorboard creaked right behind me and I started.

It was only Julian, coming out of my room and heading upstairs. "She's stable for now," he said before jumping the steps two at a time. I peeked inside the room. Kacey looked so peaceful in her broken body. She was still unconscious, but I wondered if I should stay with her. Leaving her down here by herself didn't feel right. What if the monster came back to finish the job? It was my duty to stand by her side at all times.

At the same time, she was asleep, and sitting by her bed wouldn't change anything. I could hear Alicia's frightened voice upstairs, and Rebecca's frantic gasps and shrieks. Curiosity got the better of me and I ran upstairs. They were all in the old master bedroom.

The scene which presented itself to me would have been ludicrous even in a horror film. It took me a few moments to understand what I saw. Rebecca was hanging from the ceiling, but not from her neck. An old rope had been stapled to the wooden beam, end to end, and was holding her waist up. Another thinner rope, or string, held her across the chest. She was horizontal, face down, her weight carried only by these two ropes. Except when I got closer, I saw it wasn't exactly a rope, or a string, but a wire, and...barbs?

Of course, that was why she was shrieking in pain. A rusty length of barbed wire was keeping her from crashing to the floor. Each sharp end was digging into her chest, and any time she moved, it lacerated her flesh further. Rings of blood had formed around each entry point.

Alicia and Ellis hovered around her waving their arms, trying to figure out how to grab her without hurting her even more, but anytime they tried to lift her, Rebecca screamed in agony.

"How did she end up there?" I asked Melissa.

"We don't know," she said. "She says she woke up there. She went to the bathroom, went back to bed to rest, then someone grabbed her from behind, and that's all she remembers."

A chill ran down my spine. I glanced round the room. This was the first direct assault from the killer, the first truly brutal act, and it confirmed we were dealing with a vicious psychopath. Everybody shouted and nobody heard each other. Ellis was trying to impose his course of action, Julian was cursing to make room to analyse the wounds, Patrick was trying to unhook a barb from Rebecca's arm, Lottie was shouting at Ellis to shut up, and Alicia was telling Rebecca it would all be fine. Tristan didn't know where to place himself, and he looked like he might cry. Only Leon, Melissa, Violette, Tilly, and myself were watching quietly.

I suddenly saw Leon under a different light. He was a master at concealing his true self. Could it truly go this far? Why didn't he seem to care about Rebecca's pain? In all the years, he never showed remorse when I came back home from prison. He didn't contribute at all in the search for the can of petrol. I'd never seen a sign which betrayed a sadistic nature, but he fitted the profile of those bloodthirsty serial killers we see in television series and films. The ones no one suspect as psychopaths until their horrific crimes are made public. What would his motive be, though? It struck me that those psychopaths we see in fiction didn't always need a reason. The clue was in the descriptor: bloodthirsty.

The storm of noises finally got to me and I walked up to the rope. "Does anyone have a knife?" I shouted louder than them.

That brought some much needed silence. Julian handed me a pocket knife.

"Wait a minute," said Ellis. "What are you going to do? This may not be clever, Charlie."

I sawed at the rope regardless. Rebecca needed to come down; leaving her up there while they all made up their mind was ludicrous.

"Patrick," I said, since he was standing by Rebecca's floating feet, "hold her legs, will you?"

He did what I said, and when the rope gave in at last, he held her up so that the angle didn't force the barbs deeper into her skin.

"Okay," Julian said, "I'll grab her shoulders, and you grab her around the waist," he told Ellis. "At the count of three we'll lift her up, and Alicia, you pull the wire down, got it? One, two, three–"

Rebecca's scream could have pierced through other dimensions. Alicia had to tug at the wire several times before it came loose of her flesh. Julian, Ellis, and Patrick carefully laid her down on the old bed, lifting up a cloud of dust as she hit the covers. Julian gave her some comforting words and asked Alicia to get his bag of medical supplies from downstairs.

Rebecca's skin was wet and sticky, the dust forming black streaks across her cheeks and forehead. She kept going from deathly pale to red hot, and she alternated between dreamy moans and labour-like screams.

"It's okay," Julian said, crouched by the bed and examining her arm, "Alicia will come back with some pain killers and you'll feel better in no time." He winced as he lifted her sleeve up to her shoulder.

Tristan appeared at her side and gently took her hand, but she snatched it away immediately. "*You* do not touch me, you filthy weasel," she shouted, anger – or hatred – twisting her features. Her eyes looked larger, blacker than usual. "I'll tell Flynn to gouge your eyes out if you try this again."

Poor Tristan backed out slowly, holding his hands up. Melissa and I exchanged a look, and I could see she agreed; Rebecca had lost it. The pain, the grief, or something else had gotten to her.

"There's something on the barbed wire," Patrick said, lifting it up to the light so he could have a better look. "Some type of yellow, or green, substance."

Julian stood up instantly and studied the barbs. He smelled it, then looked at it some more. "I've never come across it before," he said, "but it's definitely something that's been added and brushed onto the barbed tips, and if it's poison, it would explain the look of her wounds and how she's already feverish. It can act very quickly, it went straight into her bloodstream."

Rebecca kept writhing on the bed, making a mess of the covers and sheets and uncovering the heavily stained mattress underneath.

She was in agony, and I wished Alicia would hurry back up already; she needed some type of relief. I hoped Julian had something stronger than paracetamol or ibuprofen in his bag.

Alicia returned at last, and Julian struggled to get Rebecca to swallow the pills. She wouldn't open her mouth for him, and once she attempted to bite his hand off. In the end Ellis had to hold her down while Patrick held her mouth open, and he prevented it from shutting by placing his wallet in between her teeth.

"Don't you have a syringe or some type of sedative?" I asked Julian.

He shot me an angry look. "I didn't pack for *this*, did I? If someone had warned me I'd need to hold a one-man impromptu A&E department, yes, I would have packed the necessary equipment."

I felt foolish. I hadn't meant it as a reproach, but I could see why it had been taken as one. He had more pressure on his shoulders than any of us; not only did he have to deal with the trauma and stress of the situation, but we all expected him to care for the injured. He was the only medical person here, so what else were we to do? But even with all the knowledge in the world, without the right equipment he was powerless.

With Ellis and Patrick holding her still, Rebecca slowly calmed down. Her eyes were half open, and her mouth whispered unformed words. The exhaustion must have done it, for it hadn't been long enough for the pills to take effect. She was still sweating profusely, and all Julian could do was wipe her face with a rag, clean her wounds, sew them back up, and wait.

"Why does she get such a cruel end?" Ellis asked as he let go of her. "Killian died quickly, Flynn too, Kacey may still make it, and I get they were probably targeted randomly, but the killer didn't go out of his way to make them suffer like he did here. He singled her out. Like Mother."

"I don't know," I said, "but everything seems to come back to Timothy, and remember a few Christmases ago, when she was really mean to Lottie?" I didn't want to repeat what she'd said, but the words echoed in my mind. *You always gave the boy too much independence, you basically neglected him. You had it coming.* I had never felt so uncomfortable in my life. It was like she'd opened a tap and the hurtful words had flowed out unhindered. She'd gone on to say things like she'd failed to keep Timothy safe and it was her own fault. If she hadn't allowed him to play outside the house unsupervised, it would never have happened.

"Gosh, I'd forgotten about that," Alicia said. "The killer has a long memory, if that's it."

"More likely it's about her statement to the police, if it has anything to do with Timothy," Leon said. "Well, before she retracted it."

The thought that Leon *would* know what went on in the killer's mind came automatically to me. My subconscious appeared to be certain it was him.

I supposed he had a point. Her statement had been on a Friday, and on the following Monday, she'd retracted everything. It turned out the police had made a mistake in protocol – they hadn't waited for a child psychologist's assessment before taking her statement – and it had been erased from the file, as if it had never happened.

I had been eleven at the time, Rebecca twelve, and the attention from the media had affected me more than the statement itself. I hadn't truly grasped the meaning of it, so it had never marked me as much as it had everyone else. To me, her insensitive and outright abusive comments from a few years ago were more traumatic, and constituted a better reason for anyone, let alone Patrick and Lottie, to resent her.

"If that's what we're all thinking," Ellis said, "how is there still a doubt in anyone's mind that this is Patrick's work? Or Lottie's, I suppose, though I think we can all agree it's a man who lifted Rebecca up onto the rope."

Even for a man it would be a challenge, I thought, regardless of Rebecca's small build.

"Who else could hold a grudge so fiercely after all those years?" Ellis went on.

"It doesn't have to be someone who's out for revenge," I said, sensing Leon's eyes on me to my left. "It could be a psychopath who wants blood for the sake of blood, and who's using Timothy's death as a justification for his crimes."

To me, it was the only possible explanation. Not because I didn't believe Patrick capable of doing it, but because I didn't feel it in my guts. It just didn't fit. Basic revenge would be too obvious, too big, and he was cleverer than that. Same for Lottie, plus she had too much empathy to cause anyone pain willingly.

"If we had someone in the family who wanted blood for the sake–" Ellis stopped himself mid-sentence as steps resounded in the hallway. We all froze. Someone was coming up the steps. Slowly, one step after the other. *Thump. Thump. Thump.*

I glanced around the room. Everyone was here, around me, including Julian who hadn't visited Kacey for a little while. It couldn't be Kacey; even if she'd woken up, she was too battered to get out of bed. Surely?

The steps continued. Why so slow? I wished someone would go and see to get it over with, but I could not move my feet. Patrick's hand disappeared behind his back and returned with the gun. He cocked it. In that moment, I was glad he had it.

The steps merged into the hallway, came closer and closer, still at a snail's pace, and I held my breath as a figure appeared in the doorway.

Granny. It was only Granny. "What's with all the noise?" she said at the same time as a general sigh of relief breezed through the room – except for Rebecca, who was out of it, half awake half delirious.

Granny looked like she'd just woken up from a long night's sleep, white frizzy hair sticking in all directions, and it was mid-afternoon by then. She saw Rebecca on the bed, and stepped forward. "What's happened?"

I couldn't bear to hear it all again, so I volunteered to fetch some damp cloths to help clean Rebecca and cool her down. Julian nodded.

"I'll go with you," Melissa said, and we left the room as Ellis hurried to Granny's side.

We went down to the kitchen to get some cloths from the under sink cupboard, couldn't find any there, so we made our way to the bathroom. Melissa was oddly silent, and so was I. Every muscle in my body, every sinew, was stretched taut. I could not do small talk right now, and Melissa never did. I just needed to be away from that room. The damp and mould combined with Rebecca's sweat and eleven people's breaths had made the air thick to inhale. It felt as if Rebecca's fever was airborne. Coming downstairs, where it was chilly, was like a breath of fresh air – which it was, thanks to the fireplace's draughts.

In the bathroom, I bent down to look for tea towels, microfibre wipes, or any type of cloth which would keep Rebecca cool and clean. I found some flannels, and when I stood back up to place them under the tap, Melissa was a few inches from my face.

We stared into each other's eyes for a few moments, still without a word. I could feel her breath on my chin, smell the earl grey tea she'd had earlier, see every dark speck in her ice blue eyes. Her long brown hair encased her face like an angel's. Her lips were apart, luscious and a dark pink.

She leaned forward ever so slightly, and I kissed her. My body relaxed in one sudden wave of exhilaration. I wrapped my arms around her narrow waist and gave myself fully to her. I was hungry for her lips and tongue, and she reciprocated the fervour.

Without knowing it, this was exactly what I needed. I'd been so anxious ever since Christmas Eve, before all the madness even started, and the tension had built up until this moment. It felt so good it was almost scary. How could we find so much joy in each other, in this forbidden pleasure, with everything else happening around us?

In the heat of the moment, I still had the presence of mind to remove my ring. The guilt dampened my fire, but not by much, because I was ravenous for her skin.

I unbuttoned her jeans and buried my hand underneath. She gasped when my fingers made contact, and so did I. She gripped me tight, and it felt so good to be held with such passion. Felt so good to give someone else intense pleasure. I'd forgotten.

I lost the notion of time. I did check at some point that the door was closed, but I was so enraptured by Melissa I couldn't bring myself to care about being caught. I couldn't believe we hadn't done it sooner. Beyond that, where did this passion come from? I had no idea she had it in her.

The door suddenly opened, the click of the latch echoing against the bathroom's tiled walls. But it didn't open fully, just a smidgen, and remained ajar. We froze. My heart hammered so hard against my chest it hurt.

I could see the opening in the mirror's reflection. With the light on inside, and the hallway being dark, the gap was pitch black. I couldn't see anything, but after a second, I heard clothes rustling, a few steps walking away, and then nothing.

It occurred to me that if the person didn't come in after seeing what we were doing, they may be the killer. I rushed to the door and poked my head out, but the hallway was empty. I checked in the airing cupboard and the snug, in case he'd quickly hidden to avoid detection, but I saw nobody. I returned to the bathroom and didn't bother closing the door.

There was awkwardness in Melissa's eyes, but also a sort of satisfaction. A newfound familiarity, the same expression I probably wore myself.

"Who do you think that was?" I asked. "Leon would have stormed in, surely?"

She winced. "I'm not so sure. He could stew and sulk for hours before he decides to bring it up."

I realised she was right. It would be his style not to confront us right away, to wait for the right moment, to think of the right way to mention it. Which was why I believed him to be the killer.

At least, we knew it wasn't Kacey. A pang of guilt struck me. I was a monster. How could I do this to her, while she was fighting for her life?

"He'll kill me when he finds out, if he hasn't already," Melissa said. She leaned against the sink and crossed her arms. "Or worse. He'll make me pay in a way that will somehow be worse than killing me. The real Leon isn't the same you all know."

I scoffed at that. "Trust me, I know." Memories of the worst night of my life surfaced: the police storming in, my hesitation, the look on Leon's face. My foolish hope that he'd do the right thing. Even when I was in prison, and I hadn't heard a single word from him, I thought he'd do the right thing. I'd been blind to the real Leon before then, but no longer. "So your marriage has been struggling?" I asked.

She shrugged. "It never really thrived, so I wouldn't say we're struggling more than usual. But I am getting to the end of my rope. I've come to realise I deserve to be out of a stale relationship, and to feel what I just felt with you. There's never been passion with Leon."

No wonder, I thought, if she was gay. But she might be bisexual. "What pushed you over the line?"

I was fishing for clues as to whether he'd lied about where he was on the twenty-second, but didn't want to be open about it because she may be involved.

She turned her head to me but didn't say anything right away. Then, "I'm getting to the age where I need to have children soon, or it will be too late. Well, too late for me. And I realised I didn't want Leon to be the father of my children."

I moved to place the flannels in the sink and she shifted away, towards the towel heater. I ran the cold tap. "I think you're making the right choice, for what it's worth," I said. "Kacey and I have been struggling, and this debacle isn't helping. She didn't want to come this year. I basically dragged her, because..." I paused as I placed the flannels under the cold water. "Because I have that foolish expectation that one day I'll get along with my family, and I'll enjoy a family holiday the way I imagine it."

Melissa didn't say anything.

"Silly, right?" I went on. "The only thing I've ever wanted was to have a good time with my family, playing games, eating too much food, laughing, going for long walks and coming back in for a hot chocolate by the fire. The setting here is ideal, and I like the idea of a large family. But it never turns out that way with the Morrisons, does it?" I shook my head. "Kacey hates my parents, she hates Granny, Rebecca, Flynn, Killian, and she has no particular love for anyone else, so every trip to see them is a torture for her. I can't blame her. Same for me. The disappointment and let down every time just doubles the pain from all the drama. Now she says I deserve all the pain they give me, because I don't learn from the past and I keep looking for it. But it's not just the family."

I wrung the water out of the flannels. Melissa was still silent, which encouraged me to keep talking. She watched me in the mirror.

"We've been growing apart," I continued. "She's been spending more time with her friends, we haven't been as intimate, and I've been busy with work. We can't seem to be able to talk without fighting anymore. I've been thinking about divorce."

I dumped the flannels in the sink and turned to face Melissa. "And now... I made her come here." My voice choked up, and I could feel the tears coming all the way from my neck and up my throat. "And she may not make it, and even if she does–" The sobs swallowed my voice and Melissa hugged me.

∽

LATER ON THAT AFTERNOON, Rebecca died from her wounds. It left no doubt in Julian's mind that the barbed wire had been poisoned. Instead of stoking our desire for revenge and finding a way to escape, this new death, the brutality of it, beat us down. I, for one, could not find the energy to fight on. What was the point? It was clear we were all going to die at some point before the killer was done with us. Our fate had been announced on the day of our arrival with the graves, and a body would fill each one of them. There were more of us than there were graves, but any hope of being one of the survivors left me when I understood the meaning of the book I received.

Gatsby was murdered. The killer had every intention to give me the same fate, and suspecting Leon didn't reassure me in the slightest. My days – hours – were numbered.

I spent a couple of hours by Kacey's side, waiting for her to wake up, but she didn't. She looked peacefully asleep, and more than once I envied her. What I wouldn't give to sleep through the next few days and not be a witness to my own murder.

Alicia announced dinner, so I went downstairs despite the total absence of hunger. We all sat around the dining table, too few of us left to fill every chair. My brain counted them without my prompting. Eleven, and five empty chairs. With Granny gone back to bed and Kacey still unconscious but alive, there were thirteen of us left.

Alicia had laid some plates with cheese and cold leftovers from Christmas day. I nibbled on a cracker; I thought it less likely that crackers would be poisoned, as opposed to, say, turkey stuffing or a mince pie. I glanced around the table. The person who would rob me of my life was here, putting a piece of cheese in his mouth, faking grief. My gaze kept coming back to Leon, like metal to a magnet. He was the only one who seemed to be eating hungrily, his plate full of turkey, sausage rolls, pigs in blankets, and mince pies. Melissa, next to him, had an empty plate and a small piece of cheddar in her hand.

I turned to Tilly next to me. "Who left the master bedroom after Melissa and I left?"

"Almost everyone," she replied after a sip of water. "Julian told us to give Rebecca some room, and we all needed some fresh air anyway."

"So Julian stayed with Rebecca?" I asked.

Tilly shook her head. "Rebecca was stable at the time, she'd fallen asleep, so he went to check on Kacey."

"Who stayed behind, then?"

"Alicia and Granny. I don't know how long, I left too."

"Not Ellis?"

She turned to look at me straight in the eyes. "Why does it matter?"

Because if a man stayed behind he can probably be safely ruled out, but I wasn't about to reveal my sin to her now. I shrugged. "I'm trying to paint a picture of what everyone is doing when I'm not there to see it."

She returned her attention to the plate. "Uncle Ellis stayed at first but then I heard him say he'd go and prepare clothes for Granny."

Nothing she said added suspicion to one person in particular, but it also didn't exonerate Leon. At some point I'd need to share my theory with someone.

"Right," Ellis said loudly, "let's go over who was left alone with enough time to hoist Rebecca onto a rope, after we came back from the explosion."

Julian sucked air through his teeth. "It was chaos. You and I rushed Kacey inside and I did what I could to limit the damage."

"Lottie, Leon, Melissa and myself didn't come in straight away," Patrick said. "We carried Flynn to a grave. Still needs to be buried. I was waiting for Rebecca to feel up to it, to say a few words first…"

"I can't remember what Rebecca did when we came back in," Ellis said.

Heads turned to Tristan. His shoulders were down, his neck bent, and he was staring at his hands on his lap. Poor lad, I thought. "She was shaken up," he mumbled. "She went up quite quickly, said she needed to be alone. I didn't insist. Didn't know what to say."

"So what did you do?" Ellis asked.

"Hey now," Alicia said. "Leave the boy alone."

"No, Alicia," Ellis said. "For all we know he was alone with Rebecca on the second floor, where the master bedroom is. If he didn't do it, then how come he didn't see who did?"

Tristan took a second to reply. "I went to the sitting room. Tried to process what was happening."

"It's true," Violette said. "I saw him. I kept busy in the kitchen, washed the dishes, put some food away, tidied up. I had to be doing something, to keep myself from panicking."

"I was with Kacey the whole time," I said, in case it hadn't been obvious to everyone. "Tilly and Alicia were with me most of the time."

Ellis' gaze fell on Patrick. "What did you do when you came back from the graves?"

"Lottie and I went to our room. Tilly came to see us. Lottie checked on Kacey every now and then. Didn't feel like we were welcome anywhere outside our room."

"Same for us, really," Leon said. "We went to the car to pick up some things before coming back in, but then we just stayed in the safety of our room. We talked, trying to figure out who it could be."

"And you, Alicia?" Ellis asked.

"Like Charlie said, I was with Kacey most of the time. Went down to help Violette in the kitchen at some point."

"And you?" Patrick asked Ellis. "After you rushed Kacey in? Nobody said you stayed in the room to look after her."

"I went outside to look for clues. Someone designed an elaborate system to make that petrol catch fire. I thought there might be some type of clue, a sign that may point to who it was. I was furious, I couldn't stay cooped up inside."

"I'm not sure what the point of these interrogations is," Patrick said. "Obviously the killer is going to offer a plausible lie, so unless one of us has seen something suspicious, we're not going to stumble upon the answer by talking around this table."

"The point," Ellis said, "is to try and trip up the psychopath and establish who was alone when Rebecca was in her room, and therefore had the freedom to do what he did to her."

"Right," Patrick replied, "so we've established you were alone for most of that time."

I could see the anger build up in Dad's eyes.

"And we've established you were alone with Lottie for most of that time, which makes a lot of sense if you're working together," he said. "Even for a strong man like you, it must be hard to lift Rebecca's limp body onto that rope, but it would be a lot easier with Lottie's help."

"Stop it," Tilly said. "I know you have your issues, but stop accusing them. My parents are *not* responsible for this."

Ellis looked at her like he would an injured puppy. "Of course you're not going to suspect them, Tilly. I'm not asking you to share my suspicions, but whether you like it or not, they are the most likely culprits. No one can deny it."

I was burning to expose my theory, to put Leon on the stand, but I also had this feeling of impending disaster if I were to voice any of it. Not only was the entire family biased in his favour, but I had no evidence other than knowing what kind of person he truly was.

"Who else was alone, then?" Alicia asked. "Leon and Melissa were together."

"Which doesn't exonerate them," I said, unable to restrain myself. I stared at Leon, hoping Melissa would understand I wasn't actually suspecting her.

"Exactly," Alicia said. "Julian was mostly with Kacey, but he did leave every now and then to get medical supplies and look for substitutes and whatnot."

Julian cast a sideways glance at his wife with a raised eyebrow.

"Tristan was by himself in the sitting room most of the time," Alicia went on, "and Ellis was alone outside, and nobody may have noticed him coming back in temporarily. So all the men could have done it. I'm inclined to agree with Patrick; these exercises are pointless."

"Did you hear activity in the master bedroom?" Ellis asked me. The master bedroom was right above Kacey's and my room.

I nodded. "Some steps every now and then. But Rebecca was up there and she could have been doing anything. Alicia and Julian went up to their room sometimes to get stuff. I didn't know Tristan stayed downstairs the entire time, I thought he may be with Rebecca or checking up on her every now and then. So I didn't think anything of it."

Ellis nodded.

They all ate silently for a while. I observed everyone in turn, particularly the men, and particularly Leon. One of them *knew* about Melissa and me, yet they were keeping it to themselves. They weren't even looking at me. Leon caught my stare at one point, and immediately looked away, as if embarrassed. As much as I was convinced he was the one, if he knew about his wife's infidelity with his own sister, that was not the look I would see in his eyes. I kept scanning faces, and caught Patrick's gaze on me. He was almost squinting, and I guessed he was studying me just as I was studying him.

Or perhaps he was the one who knew.

"Are you–" came Ellis' shocked voice as he stood up to have a better look at Leon's hands. They were concealed below the table. "Are you playing a *game*?" He looked up in disbelief. "How can you possibly be playing a game at this moment in time?"

Leon brought his phone up above the table and lifted the other hand, palm up. "Just a way to distract myself, to think of other things. Is that criminal?"

"Almost!" Ellis replied in a high pitched voice. "What do you think it would look like if I suggested we play cards now for the rest of the evening? Perhap open a bottle of scotch and nibble on some peanuts?"

"Actually, I think that might be needed," Julian said. "The alcohol," he added.

"The stress of possibly being killed any minute can lead to odd impulses," Patrick said, and he looked in Leon's direction. The angle of my position was such that he could've actually been looking at Melissa. "Earlier I had a craving for olives, even though I've always hated them. Everyone reacts differently."

My pulse went into a frenzy.

I could not take my eyes off Patrick.

21

TRISTAN

As soon as someone left the dinner table, I left too. I went to the cold, empty, and dark sitting room. Everybody avoids this room because that's where Killian died, and where all the troubles started, which is why I've chosen it. Where else would I go? Rebecca's corpse is still in the master bedroom, and there's no way in hell I'm going back to our bedroom. I can't be in anyone else's presence; they're all so toxic it's a torture.

It's dark outside now, has been for about an hour. I don't feel the cold anymore. Maybe it's because I'm even colder on the inside. All emotion has left me. I'm not even grieving Rebecca's death; I barely knew her, in the grand scheme of things. I do feel like all my roots have been chopped off though, and I'm left floating in a strange place filled with terribly foreign people. Rebecca may not have been the One – though at some point I thought she might be – but she was a familiar face in the unknown. She was my anchor. Now I'm faced with imminent death, possibly through atrocious suffering, and I should be scared, terrified. But I'm just empty. Numb to life.

I'm sitting on the edge of the very sofa Killian choked on. The rug under my feet still reeks of eggnog. My back is straight, my hands are flat on my lap, and I stare blankly in front of me. I'm not comfortable, but then I don't think I can ever be warm and comfortable again. I hear distant voices upstairs, some dishes clinking together in the kitchen behind me, the inglenook fireplace whistling to my right.

I see two options in front of me: I stay in this house, where everyone is dropping like flies, one by one, amongst total strangers. Trapped like a rat in a cage, at the mercy of a psychopathic killer who holds all the cards.

Or I take control of my fate, and walk away from this place. High probability of death by starvation, cold, and exposure, but a small chance of survival. Tiny, but there. I'd spend the night in the Astra Norah was found in, sheltered from the worst of the weather, and I'd make my way up the track at first light.

Above all, I'd recover control over my own life.

Control.

22

JULIAN

Julian grunts as he lifts Rebecca's limp body onto his shoulder and walks out of the master bedroom, heavy step after heavy step. As the surgeon and only medical person here, dealing with the corpses falls on him, and he didn't have the heart to ask anyone else to help him with this morbid task. Not after everything else that's happened.

He makes his way outside, braving the night's freezing cold, and drops the corpse as delicately as he can in the rectangular hole, next to Flynn's. The ground now has a thin sheet of snow, the graves looking grotesque in the landscape. Who will say a word for them now? Tristan could speak for Rebecca, but he hasn't known her all that long. It seems more appropriate for someone like Norah, or Ellis, to say a few words. He's reluctant to leave the corpses exposed overnight, though, and he doesn't see himself urging either Norah or Ellis to come out tonight for this. So he grabs the spade and covers each of them with a thin layer of soil.

As he works at this, he reflects on the waste. Two young people in the prime of their lives. Healthy as can be. If they'd been within reach of a hospital, their organs may have been salvaged. Flynn, for instance, only died of a blow to the head, some of his skin was burnt but his organs remained unaffected. In different circumstances, with the right equipment, the right timings, and in the right location, Julian could have turned these into a waterfall of money. His dealer would have killed for those. Quite literally.

He marks a pause.

His consciousness checks in, and this thinking, right there, is evidence that something is wrong with him. When– *if* he goes back home, he'll pay for this brain of his with his freedom for the rest of his life. The remoteness of this place is the only reason he's not already in jail, he's guessing. As soon as he steps into his home, the police will fall on him.

Has it all been worth it? The big house, the fancy cars, the holidays, the boys' education. The lifestyle. When their eldest asked to study in an American university, how could he say no? Alicia never questioned the viability of their lifestyle, nobody else did either; surgeons are known to earn a good living. It never occurred to them his salary wasn't *that* good. The true price of it all has finally come knocking. They'll be deprived of a husband and father, and Julian will be as good as dead, or worse, in prison. Though after they learn of what he did, of how he allowed them to afford their lifestyle, they'll probably be glad to see him behind bars. Despite the madness of his last holiday, he has found the time to appreciate his last moments of normalcy with his wife, while ignorance still allows her to look at him. He knows he needs to savour these moments, because soon they'll be gone forever.

When he goes back inside the house, everyone is gathered in the kitchen. Violette is drying her hands with a tea towel and Charlie is staring outside, but everyone else is standing around the breakfast table.

"Where were you?" Alicia asks him, and they all fall silent.

He's slightly taken aback by the tone, so he just stares at her for a moment. "I moved Rebecca's corpse outside, into one of the holes. Where did you think I was?"

"Tristan has gone missing," Patrick says. "Do you know something? Seeing as up until now, only the two of you were missing."

Julian shakes his head. "I didn't see or hear anything outside. What do you mean he's missing? Is he dead?"

"I don't think so," Ellis says. "His coat and boots are gone, so he must be outside."

"His stuff is still in his room," Leon says.

"Let's keep an eye out," Patrick says. "He's not without suspicion. We don't really know him. Why would he go outside without saying anything?"

"For a breath of fresh air?" suggests Alicia. "God knows it's needed."

"But not now," Ellis says, "not when we need to stick together and every person who chooses to be alone becomes suspicious. Julian moving Rebecca's corpse outside is fine, it needs to be done, though a heads up would have been appreciated. But we can't willingly be alone anymore, understood?"

He looks around the room. Violette nods, and Alicia and Tilly too, but Julian doesn't, and he notices Patrick doesn't either. Julian doesn't fancy having to notify someone anytime he wants to go for a piss or to look for anything which he can use to care for the injured. He understands Ellis is the natural leader in this family, but he doesn't take well after being bossed around. Patrick neither he imagines, for different and more obvious reasons.

Julian wishes he could consider all these people family, that he could care about them the same way he did his own family, but he doesn't. He's known them for well over thirty years, and yet they're dying around him and he can't bring himself to care. Each one of them holds an emotional wall around them at all times. That's just how they are. No matter how much he's tried to bond with Ellis in the past, it's like his brother-in-law is holding back, as if he's not really interested in getting closer. Violette rarely talks. Leon, Julian has always liked him, but he's uncomfortable with banter and Julian has never figured out how to break the ice without some form of banter.

He can understand why Patrick would be protective of his emotions and not open up in the context of his family. Yet despite that, Julian still managed to create more bonds with him than anyone else in the family. He likes him for what he suffered, for how he holds himself, for how he's handled the entire situation, because had he been in his shoes, he probably would not have reacted as sanely.

"So how are we going to sleep?" asks Charlie. "If we can't be alone."

"You'll have to sleep in our room," Ellis tells her. "Same for Tilly in her parents' room."

"And leave Kacey by herself?" Charlie says. "She's not dead yet, you know."

"No," Ellis says, "but she won't be much help if the killer comes into your room, will she?"

"We have a latch on the door. I'm not leaving my wife's bed tonight."

Ellis sighs. "Fine, but Tilly, you have to be with your parents."

Tilly nods silently, and Lottie wraps an arm around her. Julian feels bad for her; no teenager should have to go through this. He doesn't even want to start thinking about what kind of long term consequences this ordeal will have on her mental health.

"If Tristan comes back," Ellis continues, "well, he'll have to be with one of us. I suppose we can make room on the floor in our room," he says, looking back at Violette.

"What about Mum?" Alicia asks.

"Crap," Ellis says. "I don't know."

It sounds like Ellis doesn't like the idea of sleeping on the floor in his mother's room. Julian smiles to himself. Ellis is adamant they *have* to stay safe at all cost, but...perhaps not at the price of his own comfort.

"Our bathroom connects," Charlie says. "The ensuite, it has two doors, one in our room, and another which leads to Granny's room. If I leave both doors open, I can hear if anything happens to her."

Ellis claps his hands. "Yes, that works. Good. And like last night, we lock our doors in whichever way we can."

"I don't see how the night can go wrong," Leon says. "We should be able to have a restful night's sleep."

"Except Tristan isn't here," Alicia points out. "Shouldn't we go looking for him outside?"

"Too dangerous," Ellis says. "It was his choice to leave the house, we shouldn't let that put us all in danger."

"What if he's the killer?" Julian says. "No one's watching him right now. He could be preparing something."

"I understand where you're coming from," Patrick says, "but are we really suspecting Tristan here? I'm worried for his safety, not that he'll murder me in my bed."

"Until we know who it is," Ellis says, "we can't exclude anyone. Otherwise we'd already have locked someone up."

"Well," Patrick says, "there's nothing we can do about Tristan right now."

"Do we lock the front door tonight?" Alicia asks.

Silence. That's a delicate question, Julian thinks.

"We can't do that to him," Patrick says. "For all we know, he just went out for a walk, to clear his head. We've all done it today."

"No, we have to lock the door," Ellis says categorically. "We can't put the rest of our family in danger just because a stranger's decided to selfishly go off on his own. If he wants to come back in, he'll just have to use the knocker."

Nobody objects, and they all head to their respective bedrooms.

∽

THE NEXT MORNING, a hammering headache assaults Julian as he sits on the side of the bed. The sleep was not restful, but as far as he knows, nothing alarming occurred in the night. He thinks of taking a pill of ibuprofen, but decides against it; someone may need it more today.

Alicia is already getting dressed. "Gosh, did the last twenty four hours really happen?" she says as she sits down on the bed to put on some socks. "I feel like Christmas was weeks ago."

Julian turns away. How hard will it hit her when she makes it home at last, relieved, and she finds out her troubles have only just started? Besides Julian's imminent incarceration, she will have to sell the house and drastically alter her lifestyle. All of this at sixty years old, when people are meant to start taking things slowly and enjoying life.

"I just want to see our boys again," she says. "I *need* to see them. It's like my heart is racing faster and faster and it won't slow down until I hold them in my arms." She turns to Julian. "Do you miss them?"

He gives her a thin smile. "Of course."

All he wants, all he's been yearning for over the last ten, twenty years, has been for her to forgive him. It all started with one deal to gather enough cash for a deposit on their house, but once he'd started, he couldn't stop. Ever since that first time, he's been haunted by how Alicia would react. Now he's exhausted, no longer has it in him to wait. For a man in his position, there is not much to look forward to. Whether he meets his end in the highlands or outside, he's meeting his end imminently.

It's a foolish hope, but he can't help himself. If she does forgive him, maybe he can suffer prison, knowing his wife will stand by him. And who knows, in that extremely unlikely scenario, the world would become full of possibilities. Perhaps she'd be open to starting a new life?

But he's only too aware the odds are overwhelmingly against him; his wife will desert him, resent him, be revolted by him, the moment she learns of what he's done. And he won't blame her.

The guilt is so strong he struggles to find the energy to stand up, but the prospect of the day ahead comes to mind and he gets to his feet nonetheless.

"At least it's sunny today," he says. "Maybe Billy will come over to bring some cows into the barn, or get some hay?"

Alicia grunts. "I can't bear to just wait for something to happen which *might* rescue us. How have we gotten into this situation? I'm never going again to the middle of nowhere, holiday or not. This house is dead to me, as are all rural locations. Cities are safe. Anywhere with bloody phone signal."

Julian wants to tell her that she should be so lucky as to only have those issues in her life. He should probably come clean now. But he can't bear bringing more darkness into her life. Not yet, not now.

All night, he played the phone call in his mind which spelled an end to his life as he knew it. The dealer, the brains behind the operation, informing him there had been a leak, a mole, and that they needed to move to a different city and start over, possibly with new identities. Either that, or get caught. Law enforcement knew the hospital was involved, it was only a matter of time before they sniffed the trail all the way back to Julian.

He had been forced to make a decision which was no decision at all. He was done dwelling in the black market, done defiling corpses. And he was certainly not going to leave everything behind, move Alicia away from the city they called home, make up another lie, all to remain in danger anyway. He decided he would face the music, whatever that entailed.

And then, the day before they left to come here, he received the dreaded phone call: a voice message from someone in the police asking for a call back. He ignored it.

By now they've probably gathered all the information they need, or soon will. Only a matter of time.

Alicia heads downstairs for a cup of tea while Julian stops by Charlie's room to check on Kacey. He doesn't see Charlie at first, he just hears her sobs. He finds her collapsed on the floor on Kacey's side of the bed, face against the old wooden floorboards. A quick check on Kacey confirms what he feared; she has passed away.

"You should have come to me as soon as she..." He doesn't finish. He had expected it; Kacey was brain dead, and they don't have the equipment to keep her alive.

Charlie takes a moment to pull herself up and sit with her back against the wall's peeling wallpaper, elbows on her knees. "I only just noticed now," she says in between sobs, "a minute ago. It's all my fault."

"Don't be silly," Julian says. "You didn't cause that explosion."

"Not that, but–" She sniffs and wipes her nose with the back of her hand. Then she shakes her head and gives up on what she was going to say.

A knock comes on the door, and Melissa's head pops in. Her face turns to ashes when she realises what's happened, and they both embrace. Julian is relieved they have each other; he's not comfortable with displays of emotion and dealing with grieving people. When he's done preparing Kacey's body to be moved, he leaves the room and hears Melissa tell Charlie she must return to Leon; she left while he was in the bathroom, and he won't be happy to be left alone.

∽

JULIAN BRINGS MORE doom in the kitchen as he announces the passing of Kacey. Alicia brings him a hot cup of tea.

"We need to stay together all day until we find help," says Ellis. "Where's Charlie?"

"I left her upstairs," Julian says. "She needs some time with Kacey."

"We have to go outside and use the sunny weather to our advantage," Lottie says. "Someone may be within reach. If we shout often enough and for long enough, someone may hear us. There are deerstalkers about, right? And farmers, maybe hikers, bird watchers."

"I agree," says Alicia. "I can't stay in this house much longer."

"No news of Tristan?" Julian asks.

They all shake their head.

"We could keep an eye out for him, while we're outside," Alicia says.

"Who's missing?" Ellis looks around, scanning every face. "Charlie, Mother, Leon, and Melissa. We need to get them down here, see if Mother feels up to it today."

As he says this, loud steps coming from the staircase make the walls shake. It stops halfway down, and Leon's voice follows: "It's Melissa! Come, quick!"

Charlie, being on the same floor, makes it to the bedroom before any of us. She freezes as she sees the bed; her hands are suspended in front of her in the same position they were when she pushed the door open. Alicia wails loudly, and Lottie gasps. There are too many people in the entrance for Julian to see anything, so he peeks through the narrow gap in between the door and doorframe.

Melissa's body is sprawled across the bed's unkempt sheet and cover. With his limited view, it looks like she's having a rest, but he knows that's not right. She's not moving, and he glimpses some red stains on the pillow. "Let me through," he says immediately, pushing his way to the bed.

But there's no use. He doesn't even need to check her pulse. Her throat has been slit open and she's been dead for a few minutes. Her face is turned away from him; save for her savaged throat, she looks like she could be asleep.

He scans the room. Several people are looking away – Tilly, Lottie, Patrick – and so they should; anybody with a hint of squeamishness at the sight of blood is performing a superhuman effort by remaining in the room.

"I– I– I know what it looks like," Leon says, lifting his hands in the air. "But you *have* to believe me, I found her like this." His eyes are wide as golf balls, as if his eyelids have been glued open. "I went to the bathroom and– and she wasn't there when I came out. I went looking for her all over the house, even went to the attic and that awful master bedroom. I came downstairs looking for her. Mum, you saw me, right?"

Violette nods timidly.

"And when I came back to check if perhaps she was waiting for me here," he goes on, "I found her like this."

Charlie growls next to him, eyes puffy and red. "You monster. And why are you more afraid of our suspicion than you are sad about your wife's brutal murder?"

"I *am* sad," Leon assures her, "I'm devastated! What do you think? But I know what it looks like, and I did *not* do this."

"You are the only one who had a reason to be alone with her," Patrick says. "This is the first time we're so close to knowing the exact context of a murder, that we can actually point the finger to someone."

"But, no!" cries Leon. "Why would I kill my own wife? And why now, and not in the dead of night?"

"Who's the only one who ate heartily last night?" Charlie asks the room. "Leon. Who played a game because he was bored by what was happening around us? Leon. Who's the only one who seems to be detached emotionally from all these deaths? Leon. Did he help us find the can of petrol? Of course not. Leon has been–"

"Okay, you've made your point," says Ellis. "Let's try to look at this objectively. It does seem strange that he'd take the risk to kill her now, when he could be seen or heard, rather than during the night. She obviously died very recently, so who else could have done it? I went straight from my room, where I was with Violette, to the kitchen for breakfast, where everyone else was."

"You went to the bathroom after you came to the kitchen," Patrick says.

Ellis stares blankly at his brother. "So what?"

"So you were alone, Ellis. Wouldn't have taken long to go up the stairs, find her alone in her room, slit her throat, and come back down."

"That is ridiculous. Are you even hearing yourself? What about you? Did you go to the bathroom at any point this morning?"

"Not yet, no. I was with Lottie and Tilly all night, I came down to the kitchen with them, and I've been there ever since with one person or another."

"Actually I didn't come down with you," Lottie says. "I was in the shower. I came a few minutes later."

"There you are," Ellis says. "If you're working together, that would've been a great time for her to pay Melissa a visit in her room."

"I saw her this morning," Charlie says, tears streaming down her face as she stares at the corpse. "Not long ago at all, Julian did too. She came to check on Kacey, saw she was dead, and she comforted me. Then she said she had to go back to her room because she left while Leon was in the bathroom. I guess he was out waiting for her when she returned."

"What about you, Julian?" Ellis asks.

"Like Charlie said, I was in her room when Melissa came. I was checking on Kacey. Then I went up to the bedroom to drop my bag off and grab a mint, and I came down to the kitchen." He marked a pause, then said what everyone was thinking. "So yes, I was alone for a few minutes and could technically have done it."

"And you and Leon didn't happen to cross each other's paths?" Ellis asks.

"Seems not."

"For what it's worth," says Violette, "I came down relatively early with Ellis, and Tilly was there with me the entire time. Same for Alicia when she came down, and that would have been too early for... this...to happen."

"There's something in her mouth," Alicia says, looking at Melissa.

All heads turn to Julian. He walks around the bed, places a knee on the mattress, and extricates what seems to be a pair of underwear from inside her mouth. He holds it up pinched in between two fingers for everyone to see. Rumpled black lace.

"Are those knickers?" Alicia asks.

"What in the–" Ellis stops himself as Charlie gasps.

She takes a few steps forward to have a better look, then brings her hands to her mouth. "They're mine."

"*Yours*?" Violette says in a high pitched voice.

Julian notices something under Melissa's cheek. He gently pulls up her chin to lift her head, and picks up a small piece of paper.

"Second circle of Hell: Carnal malefactors in the bathroom," Julian reads. He looks up to meet confused and frowning faces. "Adultery," he translates, and glances at Charlie. She hasn't moved, and is just staring at the bed.

"In the bathroom?" Violette asks.

A moment of silence as everyone processes this.

Leon relentlessly massages his temples. Julian can't imagine himself in his shoes.

Ellis shakes his head. "I don't understand. Is this all a joke to that psychopath?" He looks at Patrick as he says this. "An endless string of riddles for his amusement, while killing us off one by one?"

"At the risk of looking even more like the killer to you," Patrick says, "this is not a riddle. This is an accusation. The killer is accusing Melissa of committing adultery with Charlie in the bathroom."

Heads turn to Charlie.

"Is it true?" Violette asks her daughter.

Charlie continues staring at the bed in silence. Her dyed blonde hair is oily and lifeless, with some loose strands sticking to her damp cheeks. She's nibbling on her thumb's nail in quick and repetitive movements, as if she's temporarily lost it. Julian begins to worry she's having a stroke when she speaks at last.

"No, of course not. That's exactly what the murderer wants, to make us believe things and have us kill each other. Do you seriously think anyone in this family had a hand in Timothy's death? Of course not, but that's what that sicko wants us to believe!" Her voice becomes edgy towards the end.

"Charlie," Leon says in a calm voice, removing his hands from his face, "did you sleep with my wife?"

"Again," Charlie says, lifting a hand to mark her point, "no. My wife is – was – in the house, for God's sake."

Patrick seizes Charlie's wrist while it's still up. "Your ring," he says. "It's missing."

Charlie freezes. A current passes through the room, and Julian knows they're all thinking the same thing.

He doesn't notice who moves first, but several people rush out of the room at the same time. He follows them out; they need to get to the bathroom before Charlie to prevent her from hiding the ring.

He goes for Charlie and Norah's ensuite bathroom on the same floor, along with Ellis, Violette, and Leon who were ahead of the pack, but Charlie dashes down the stairs. Julian changes course and follows Patrick and Lottie down.

By the time they reach the bathroom, Patrick and Charlie are neck and neck, and Charlie manages to snatch the ring first, but it's no longer any use hiding it.

"Oh, Charlie," Lottie says, panting.

"Anything else you want to tell us?" Patrick says as Charlie's parents and Leon reach the hallway.

"This does not mean I did anything with Melissa," she says. "I remove my ring all the time to wash my face and shower."

"*Chérie,*" Violette says softly, "how could you?"

"Mum, I–"

"Quit it, Charlie," Patrick says. "How did you know it would be in this bathroom? You have an ensuite in your room complete with a bath and shower, why in the world would you come down here to wash your face or shower?"

Charlie opens her mouth but no words come out. It stays open and distorts as the tears return. Alicia rushes to her side and lets her bury her face in her shoulder. Julian can't bring himself to feel any empathy for her. How could she do this to her own brother? He had never had a high opinion of her, but that was lower than even he thought she could go.

Leon's face is flushed. It's like his lips are wrestling against his brain, twisting and trembling. "How could you?" He can barely get the words out.

Charlie's face quickly emerges from Alicia's shoulder. Her eyes are so swollen they can't open fully. "How could I?" She gives a hysterical laugh. "Coming from you? Haaaa." She leaves Alicia's embrace. "No, that's too much." She stomps out of the bathroom and pushes past Leon.

"Come back here, Charlie," Ellis calls out, "we have to stick together, none of us can stay alone."

But she doesn't come back, or turn around. If anything, she quickens her step and slams the sitting room door behind her.

∽

Alicia moves to go after Charlie, but Julian places a hand on her arm. For a fraction of a second, it seems to him she recoils at his touch.

"I'll go," he says.

His wife hesitates, then shrugs. "If you're sure?" she adds.

Julian nods with a thin smile. She returns his smile, and she's back to being herself.

He's not certain why he wants to talk to Charlie himself, or what he can do to improve the situation. But her reply to Leon, and the way she said it, intrigued him. He suspects there's more to it than the family knows.

The air in the sitting room has a smokey tinge to it. Charlie is sitting on the sofa across from the one Killian choked on, her elbows on her knees and her face buried in her hands. She looks up briefly when Julian sits down next to her. The sofa's cold leather creaks loudly under him.

"I'm not here to judge you," he says. "I know enough about mental health to understand the unpredictable effects of extreme stress. The pressure needs a release somehow, and the way it releases isn't always the one we'd choose, or the wisest. But sometimes these things are out of our control."

She sniffs a couple of times and wipes her tears with her jumper's sleeve. "Thanks." She smacks her lips together.

They've rarely, if ever, spent time just the two of them, so the awkwardness is heavy. He's never warmed to her and she must have felt it over the years, so she must be wondering what he's doing here. To him, she's the epitome of the party animal. Thrives on attention, social interaction, alcohol-induced drama, and provoking reactions in people, her family most of all. That's the impression she gave ever since she was a teenager. He disagrees with Norah on virtually everything, but on this, he is ashamed to say they see eye to eye. However, he is willing to give her the benefit of the doubt. Without anything else to say to try and make her feel better, he goes straight to the reason he's there.

"What's the history between you and Leon? You've always made it clear you hold a grudge, that he's hurt you in some way, but you don't seem to want to put it in the open."

She lays her hands on her lap and straightens her back. "What's the point? Everyone here loves Leon and will always be biased in his favour. If I say anything against him, it will somehow be turned against me."

"Try me. It's only me here, and I promise you to be open and impartial. I want to understand what's going on. And I think you'll feel better if you get it off your chest."

She studies Julian for a moment, then sinks back in the sofa and fiddles with the lip of her woollen jumper. "Back when I was twenty. Leon was twenty-three. I was still in uni, Leon was... between things, supposedly looking for teaching work, but mostly just drifting. He called one weekend and asked if I could drive him and a mate to a party, just outside the city. I was thrilled. I'd never been invited anywhere with him before — not like that. It felt like I was finally in his circle. Like I wasn't just his kid sister."

She pauses, swiping her sleeve across her nose, her gaze slipping to her hands. "I didn't even go inside. Just waited in the car, texting, watching drunk people wander in and out of the house. After an hour or so, Leon came running out, pale as anything, told me we had to go, now. Wouldn't explain why. Just kept saying, 'Don't ask questions, just drive.' So I did."

"What happened?" Julian asks.

"The next morning, police knocked on my door. Said there'd been a theft at the party — laptop, wallet, a few other things. Someone at the party said they saw Leon with the stolen stuff, and they gave the police my license plate. That's how they ended up at my flat. I didn't understand. Then they found the laptop in my uni bag."

She goes quiet. Julian says nothing.

"I realised later — he must've stashed it in my bag before he left. He never said anything. Never asked if I got questioned. Never even checked if I was okay. Just... silence."

"Did you tell the police it was him?"

She shakes her head. "No. I froze. I didn't want to get him in trouble. I told them I didn't know how it got there, and eventually they believed me. They couldn't prove I knew it was my bag, and they had no evidence against me."

"You never actually went to prison."

"No, just arrested, taken in for questioning and held overnight, but that was enough for everyone to see me as the girl who got arrested even though I did nothing. And Leon—he just carried on. Like it had never happened."

Julian's brow tightens. "He used you."

"Yeah," she says softly. "And I let him."

"I'm so sorry this happened to you," Julian says, laying a hand on her knee.

She shrugs. "So from then on I decided to have fun and only look out for myself, because other people aren't worth fighting for. Even those you thought you knew better than anyone else."

Her story comes as a shock to Julian. He stares at the shafts of sunlight piercing through the room's dimness, and takes a moment to process everything before speaking.

"I've always been one of those people in the family you mentioned who like Leon. The Leon I know is kind, quiet, timid, eager to be helpful. A good-hearted soul who would never cause anyone any harm. The kind of guy who would rather go hungry than take food away from his friends. I've always likened him to Bob Cratchit. You know, Ebenezer Scrooge's opposite. But I'm starting to see a different Leon for the first time."

"Melissa told me the same," Charlie says. "The Leon you all see is not the real him. He's good at hiding his true self."

"It did strike me as odd that he seems so detached from everything happening around us," Julian went on. "And he went for the gun, didn't he? Maybe he doesn't think we've noticed, but he faked looking for the can of petrol, and in the end went for the gun, only Patrick was quicker. That's a side to him I didn't know. And now you tell me this."

A moment of silence follows, but the awkwardness has disappeared. Julian is also rediscovering Charlie. Talk about being misunderstood, he thinks to himself.

"Thank you," Charlie says, looking at him. Her eyes have dried at last. "For believing me, and for listening."

"Of course," he says. "Right, I can hear them behind us, they've moved to the kitchen. I'll go back, and you should come too. Ellis is right, we shouldn't be on our own if we can avoid it."

"Okay," she says but stays put for now. Julian stands up and walks away.

"Julian," she calls as he's about to open the door, "I think Leon may be the killer."

He nods. "I'll keep an eye on him."

23

NORAH

I wake up invigorated. I've slept like a well-behaved baby, straight through from midnight or so. I can't remember when that last happened, but now I feel like myself again.

Then the memories flood in, one by one. The abduction, the days of sheer misery, the cold, and then the murders. The energy leaves me in one long sigh. I'm too old for this. I want to go back home, where it's warm and the continuous traffic noise is reassuring. I stay in bed for a while, enjoying the house's soft noises of activity. A toilet flushes, someone goes down the stairs, some doors shut, upstairs and down. As long as there is nothing too loud, too sudden, then the peace continues. But for how long?

Then I hear a loud shout in the staircase, and the throng of steps which follows. Something's happened in Leon's room. Not Leon himself, he's the one who shouted, and thank God for that. I should get out of bed to go and see what happened, but I can't be asked. Pulling the covers off, swinging my legs to the side, pushing to get onto my feet; it just requires so much effort.

So much effort for what? To receive more bad news? I don't think I can take it. Depending on who the news is about.

In the end Ellis comes to me and informs me of the latest deaths.

I breathe a sigh of relief. The door to my room is ajar, and I can hear hushed tones in the hallway.

"Ellis, it sounds like there's someone behind the door," I whisper, glancing skittishly at the door.

Ellis gives me a soft smile. "Yes, they're all there, waiting for us to come out. We can't afford to be separated."

"So what's the plan now?"

"Do you think you can get up?" His eyes are filled with pity. Or concern. I see it as pity.

"I'm better today. Help me down."

He gives me his arm and I grip it. He pulls me up, and hands me my dressing gown.

"Let's try and have some breakfast, shall we?" he says, and holds my arm again even though there's no longer a point to it. "We all need some food in us, regardless of what's happening."

I snatch my arm away. "I can still walk by myself."

In the dining room, Alicia brings me a cup of tea and Ellis a plate of toast. Nobody speaks, thereby creating a morbid atmosphere. I noticed Charlie wasn't upstairs when I got out of my room, and she isn't here now. When everybody's sat down and is passing the milk and sugar and whatnot, I ask: "Is Charlie dead?"

Lottie recoils. I don't place my full gaze on her, but from the tail of my eye I can see she's loaded her eyes with loathing.

"No, Mo–" begins Ellis.

"What if we said yes?" Patrick interrupts. "Would you just go back to nibbling on your toast, with a mere shrug of the shoulder?"

I stare at the insolent child.

Now he's the one shrugging. "That's the impression you give."

"Charlie is in the sitting room," Ellis tries again. "She's…shaken by the recent events, and needs some alone time."

Alicia gets up and disappears into the hallway. She returns and says, "Still there."

"Aren't we all?" I say. They all look at me with a confused look on their face. "Shaken by the recent events," I specify, and turn to Ellis.

"Why are you allowing your daughter to disobey you? Didn't you say no one can be alone?"

He wipes his lips with a napkin, then lays it carefully on his lap. "Something else happened, that I haven't told you yet. Melissa...well..."

And he tells me of Charlie's grotesque and disgusting act of debauchery. I don't know why I let it shock me, it's nothing new with her. I am disappointed at Leon for choosing such a depraved woman for a wife – there are always early signs for these things – but fully expected it from Charlie. Yet still, to think she would do this to her own brother, and now of all times.

I realise I'm shaking with rage. My age is the only thing keeping me from storming out of the room and slapping that whore right across the face. I bring the cup of tea to my lips with difficulty, the steaming liquid threatening to spill, but the warmth nestling in my stomach calms me down.

"Do not say anything to Charlie when you see her again," Alicia says. "She's suffering enough as it is."

I stare at my daughter for a few moments. "*Can* she suffer enough? She will in hell, I suppose. If there ever was any hope for her before this Christmas, there certainly isn't now. I wonder where you've gone wrong," I add, glancing at Ellis' plate.

"And where do you think *you* will go?" Violette says in her coarse French accent.

"What was that?" I do not take my eyes off my cuppa. "I didn't understand what you said."

"*Vous n'êtes vraiment qu'une sale pétasse.*"

A scent catches my attention, and everything else vanishes. I'm back in my car's back seat, hands and feet bound, blind and wet from my own piss. The door opens and the deep modified voice tells me it's dinner time. A piece of buttered bread is shoved into my mouth. I spit it back out and throw a string of insults. A faint odour floats in the air, the characteristic odour of that person, every time they open the door.

I come back to the dining room. The scent has vanished. I try to identify it; I know it, how can I not remember what it is? Lavender? No, it's something edible. Like lemon, or chamomile, but not quite.

I look around the table. Where did it come from? Is it someone's perfume, aftershave? The reality hits me flat in the face. The murderer is around the table. Right now, as I breathe, the psychopath is looking at me. Wondering how I will respond to my daughter-in-law, but I have no care whatsoever for her. I always knew it was one of them, but...yes, it is one of *them*. Someone here killed, several times, and abducted me. Treated me worse than a dog.

Is it Patrick? There's hesitation in his eyes, and his cheek twitches when my attention falls on him. Next to him Lottie avoids my eyes. She is closest to me, so perhaps the smell came from her. But where is it now?

Ellis. He's avoiding me too. Violette is openly glaring at me. When I meet her glare, she must see that I'm distracted because she blinks and breaks the eye contact to butter her toast. Julian next to her seems focused on making sure every grain of sugar is fully dissolved in his cup.

Alicia and Leon are staring like a pair of rabbits about to bolt. Tilly looks curiously my way, as if fascinated.

It doesn't matter how long I stare at every single one of them, I can't spot a sign which would betray them. I know these people, half of them are my own children. How can I not know for certain which one it is? My instinct tells me it's Patrick, but even then, I find it difficult to believe.

"One of you is a murderer," I say. "One of you is a dangerous psychopath who will burn in hell for eternity for murdering your kin. One of you is a raging coward. Won't you even stand up and assume the responsibility?" I try to add as much venom as I can in my voice, to elicit a reaction, but my words fall flat.

An unwelcome wave of emotion seizes my throat. I place a hand on my lips. "Oh, my children. How have we come to this?"

My throat has clasped shut and no more words will come out. I desperately try to keep the tears in, so as not to show any sign of weakness.

"Are we just going to sit here in silence and not point out how it's most likely partly her fault?" Lottie asks the table. "Whatever the killer's motivations, she shaped every person here, in one way or another, and to some degree. Over the years she fed conflicts, poured buckets of fuel over fire, emotionally abused her children, deliberately lied to law enforcement."

"Hey," Ellis says, raising a hand, "that's going a bit far."

"It's fact, Ellis," Patrick says. "If she's to be angry with anyone, she should start with herself."

"You would know," Ellis says, "wouldn't you? I've said all along you know the killer's mind better than anyone because it's yours, and here you are telling us what motivated the killer as *fact*."

I put my cup of tea down on the saucer a bit harder than intended, and the clink turns all heads in my direction. "I'm going back to bed."

I quietly dare anyone to stop me, but no one does.

24

ELLIS

I'm sweating when Julian, Leon, and I come back from carrying the corpses to the temporary graves. The others are in the dining room, where we left them, and Charlie is now at the table. Nothing happened while we were out. Anytime I enter a room, I have this dread that I'll see a corpse, or blood, or something which signals another death. I hated leaving Violette in the dining room, especially with Patrick there, but Alicia stayed with her and I trust her. Besides, Tilly was also with her, and as monstrous as he is, I doubt he'd go so far as to kill in front of a child.

"Violette," I call, "can you come with me?"

"Where are you going?" Patrick asks.

I think about fobbing him off; I don't owe him an explanation. But as much as I mistrust him, I'm not hundred percent certain he's the murderer, and if it were the other way around, I'd want to know where he's going too.

I gesture to my shirt. "I need to change, so Violette will come with me so I'm not by myself." The shirt's sweaty patches are cold against my skin. Hate the feeling.

"We'll go outside as soon as you're ready," Alicia says, lifting her head from her embrace with Charlie. It seems she's taken on the role of mother to my daughter. Distasteful, but in the circumstances, I don't complain. Saves me or Violette the trouble. I can barely look at her right now.

Violette sits on the bed while I change. It pains me that she has to go through this nightmare, and I'm powerless to take her away. The least I can do is not leave her side again; I can at least shield her from immediate danger.

"Where *did* we go wrong?" she asks, wringing her hands together. "How could our daughter do this to her own brother?"

"I don't think it has anything to do with us, darling. I think people are born with their own personality and characteristics, and parents can shape them, but only to a certain extent. Charlie has always been rebellious, always got a kick out of making our life miserable. It's in her nature to create drama, nothing we can do about that."

She continues twisting her fingers together. I sit next to her and take one hand in mine. "Honey, don't beat yourself up. Our job was always to keep her fed and safe. We did that. Now she's an adult, it's all on her. Not you." I deposit a kiss on her cheek.

"Still," she says, "we can't be entirely blameless."

If nothing else, I hate Charlie for doing this to my wife. She's the most wonderful woman I know, the best mother a child could have ever asked for, and that daughter of ours has managed to make her feel like a failure. I can't stand to see her hurting like this.

"Then how do you explain Leon?" I say. "He's a model son, isn't he? They have the same parents, received the same education, same parenting, same environment, and yet they couldn't be more different. Doesn't that confirm beyond the shade of a doubt what I've just said?"

She raises an eyebrow. "We didn't really treat them the same. You said it yourself, Charlie never listened to us, she was so difficult, so we were always angry with her. Leon was a good boy, so we gave him more love. Perhaps we were too hard on her."

"Don't," I say, squeezing her hand. "Don't you dare blame yourself. How were we to react to her nonsense? Were we meant to just shrug and smile when she'd make a scene for no reason whatsoever?

Remember when she came home from school one day, I think she was five, and she drew all over her bedroom's wall? She kept laughing when we told her off. At such a young age she was already a b– pain. How is any parent meant to react to that without losing their shit?"

She gives a heavy sigh. I kiss her again on her hair and stand to button up my shirt. When I'm ready, we stop by Mother's room. I open the door and pop my head in.

"We're going outside to look for help and phone signal, and I'd like you to come with us."

"Not a chance, Ellis," Mother says. "I'm staying right here until we can leave this God forsaken place."

"Then someone will stay with you. I'm not leaving you alone, Mother."

"If you're all going out, then there won't be anyone left to kill me, will there?"

I shake my head. "It's not that simple. Not only does the murderer seem to always manage to seize every opportunity to strike unseen, but we're not even sure there isn't someone else on the grounds. Leaving you alone would be the perfect opportunity for someone else to come in unhindered."

She waves me away with contempt. "Then lock the door."

I turn to Violette and roll my eyes. "Fine, have it your way. We'll see you later."

25

PATRICK

It's a sunny day, and with the cold breeze and warm sunshine on my face, our predicament doesn't feel as dire as it has until now. Surely, we'll get out soon. Somehow. There are no walls holding us in, the view is open to the skies, and there are people out there, somewhere.

Alicia comes to me and matches my stride. "Do you think Mum will ever understand her role in all this?"

I look at my sister. There are bags under her eyes, and her skin looks drier than I expected, more wrinkled around the eyes and mouth. The warm blue eyes, which have always reassured me as a boy, now reflect her age. I assume it's the stress of our predicament exacerbating everything. A rush of affection seizes me as I think of her getting older, as I think fondly on our young years, my only ally when growing up.

When I think about her eternal naivety.

"No, of course not. Mum does not admit wrongdoing, and especially not about something this grave. And it's understandable; how could she live with herself if she recognised her abusive and hurtful behaviour and its consequences?"

She sighs and shakes her head. "I don't want to think of this for now. Or anything going on in there." She points at the house behind us.

"How are your boys getting on?" I ask.

That does the trick. Her gaze travels far away as a mother's love erases some of her wrinkles. "Cameron is loving it in Thailand, studying the corals and marine life. The charity has no plan to call him back for now, and it turns out I'm very happy about that."

"Yes, he wrote to me a couple of months ago. He seems to be thriving."

"He is so grateful for your help getting the job, as I am." She places a hand on my arm.

"I'm just glad he's enjoying himself, he deserves it. Where's Edward now?"

"The last I heard he was in Costa Rica. I think his gap year may extend into a year and a half, but I'll never discourage him from travelling."

Tilly joins us, and Alicia asks her about school.

When we get to the top of a hill, we shout ourselves hoarse. It feels good to let it out, to release the tension and pressure which has been building up. The hills are a pale green at this time of year, verging on yellow, and there are patches of snow here and there. The trees are brown and skeletal, and the landscape is generally bare, but the sunlight adds a quality which would make a swamp look vibrant. The white-capped mountain in the distance, with the deep blue loch at its feet, is majestic. I can almost smell the pine trees bordering the water.

"Signal!" Tilly shouts. "Oh, it's gone. But I had a bar for a second. That's hope, right?"

Everyone agrees, and for the first time we can see the light at the end of the tunnel. We all take our phones out and frantically check for signal. Alas, Tilly's bar must have been an anomaly, because it never returns. No one has heard our shouting, even when we repeat the attempt at the top of another hill. We spot a few stray sheep in the distance, and Julian jokes about having dinner if we ever run out of food in the house, but there are no shepherds in sight.

We are forced to return to the house with only the tiniest glimmer of hope that perhaps someone's heard us and will call on us at some point before the end of the day.

26

ELLIS

As we step into the house, the smoke alarm is blaring. The air is filled with smoke and it reeks of burnt food. Julian rushes into the kitchen; I run into the hallway, and stop dead.

My mother, mostly concealed by her large dressing gown, is sprawled over the last few steps of the staircase, her bloodied head resting against the wall and preventing the rest of her body from sliding onto the floor. I want to crouch next to her, to check if she's still breathing, but I'm terrified. I can't put it into words. It's as if a skyscraper has collapsed at my feet, as if a part of me has just died, as if the planet has stopped spinning. My stomach feels as if it's in a free fall.

"Toast in the oven," Julian says as he returns from the kitchen. "Did someone place it there, and turn the oven on before we left?"

He notices our faces, follows the gazes, then swears loudly. He steps forward, bends down, and shakes his head. Then he lifts her head, studies her body, and glances at the stairs and walls. "It looks like she died from falling down the stairs – she wasn't bludgeoned beforehand. The head wound is consistent with the stains on the steps and the wall."

"Do you think she came down when the smoke alarm went off, and fell by accident?" Patrick asks.

Julian shrugs. "She could technically have been pushed, but an accident's one plausible explanation. Oh," he adds, looking at her feet.

I wake up at last, and come to stand next to him. I notice, like him, that her left foot is suspended a few inches above the nearest step, held by a thread from her beige tights which runs up the stairs. It is still stretched taut, so we follow it up.

It's wrapped around an old nail sticking out from a floorboard at the edge of the top step. It has been deliberately pulled to trip up someone. I'm too stunned to speak, so Julian tells everyone. He unwraps the thread, and her foot makes a soft thud as it drops down.

They speak, but it's all a confused buzz of white noise to my ears. My mother is dead, her head split open on the ancestral family home's steps. None of the other deaths felt this way. This is like... As if my life energy had lived inside her, and now that she's gone, I am drained. I realise I never thought the murderer would go so far as to kill her. I naively thought the abduction would be as far as he'd dare go.

I look down from the stairs at the rest of them. Patrick is rubbing his face in the hallway. Alicia is sobbing into Julian's shoulder. Violette is looking at me, then at the floor, and back at me. I realise she's trying to get to me but Mother's leg is in the way, and her tight skirt is preventing her from stepping over. Instead I come down to the ground floor.

She gives me comforting words, but no words will ever fill this new void inside. I knew she'd die eventually, obviously, but this is so unexpected and brutal. And I'd never allowed myself to imagine her death, thinking I'd deal with it when it came to it. Now that it has come, I don't think I can.

Violette takes me into the dining room while they clear the corpse. Alicia and Tilly are sitting next to each other, holding hands. Violette tells me Charlie is cleaning up the mess, and I visualise the blood on the old plaster and wooden steps and a wave of nausea seizes my stomach. I manage to keep it in, but I must have gone pale because Violette places the fruit bowl in front of me and goes to fetch me a glass of water.

"Patrick," I say when she returns. "Where is he? He's not carrying her body, is he, so where is he?"

"I'm here," Patrick says, behind me. He's leaning against the corner of the room, arms folded in front of him. Lottie is there too.

Now would've been a good time for him to slip out and prepare his next move; everybody is too shocked or distracted to keep an eye on each other. But he didn't even try to be alone. I hate it, but perhaps it's not him. Then who?

A part of my mind wants to know, but the rest is too exhausted, or uninterested. I suppose it's my survival instinct telling me to watch for the killer. That and the desire to keep Violette safe. Charlie and Leon too, I suppose, but they need to look out for themselves. I don't have it in me to worry for anyone other than Violette right now.

∽

Some time passes while I'm in a daze. Julian and Leon return from outside, Charlie too from cleaning up, and then Violette goes to the kitchen. I hear hushed tones coming from the kitchen, someone urging someone else to do something, they refuse, "Not now" I hear Violette say. Alicia hears it too; she gets up and stands in the doorway.

"What's going on here?" she asks.

"Might as well, now," I hear Julian say.

"Let's go into the dining room," Charlie says.

"For the record," Leon says as they emerge into the room, "I didn't think it was a good idea to share this with everyone. I said it should go straight to the bin."

"What are you talking about?" Patrick asks.

"This," Julian says, holding up a folded letter.

He shows it to Alicia. Once she's read it, she shakes her head. "Unnecessary."

Patrick approaches and reads over Alicia's shoulder. His face drops, then he sends me a look which leaves no doubt the content is about me.

Alicia takes a few steps in my direction.

"Are you sure that's a good idea?" Leon asks.

"We have no choice now," Alicia snaps back. "We can't just ignore it any longer."

She hands me the letter. It's been typed up, so no chance of recognising the handwriting. There are only two quotes, and no explanations. They read:

"STATEMENTS FROM MEMBERS of the family were contradictory. Mrs Alicia Powell and her husband swore that Mrs Powell's parents were away to visit her uncle in Dundee for the entire day. The same was supplied by the victim's father, Mr Patrick Morrison. When the victim's grandparents, Mr and Mrs Richard Morrison, were questioned, they told the police they were with their son, Mr Ellis Morrison, all day, in his house. This was corroborated by Mr Ellis Morrison, his wife, as well as their uncle, in whose house Mrs Powell claimed her parents had spent the day."

"IT WOULD BE a shame if something happened to Timothy and it brought reality crashing down on you, to show you that not everything in life goes well, not everything is rosy and works out miraculously well. I know it's hard for you to believe, I mean, what ever goes wrong for you? But no one can be so divinely lucky all the time, Patrick."

MY EYES STAY on the piece of paper even after I am done reading. I remember the first quote from a newspaper article. I know the second passage quotes my words from a lifetime ago, but have I really said this, or is the murderer making some of it up? Could I have been so heartless as to bring his innocent child into our feud?

"Where did you find this?" Patrick asks.

"On the kitchen table," Charlie replies. "Under an orange."

"I'd almost forgotten," Lottie says. "The wording, that is. Not the threat. That I never forgot."

"Who said this?" Tilly asks.

All heads turn to me. I refuse to say anything.

"Ellis," Lottie answers for me. "In the sitting room. On Boxing Day."

"Did you really, Dad?" Charlie asks.

I can't help but scoff. "You're one to talk." I can feel the oozing judgement in everyone's eyes. "I was drunk, you might remember, and I can't remember mentioning the child specifically, but even if I did, I never meant if something deliberate was done, only if an *accident* happened."

"Oh, well, that's much better," Patrick says, lifting his hands up. "Thanks for clarifying that, brother. I'd been seething for years, wondering how you could possibly say something like that and then not be involved in my son's murder, but now that you've clarified you only meant if an *accident* happened, my mind is at peace."

"Look," I say, "I recognise it was an incredibly insensitive thing to say, I shouldn't have done so, but that does not mean I was involved in Timothy's death."

The mention of his name is like a shower of ice has crashed upon the room.

"No?" Patrick says. I can feel the anger building in him. "What about the first quote on there? Why did you and Mum and Killian all lie to the police?"

I stare at him in silence for a moment, making every effort to keep my face as neutral as possible. "We didn't. We told them the truth."

I glimpse Patrick's right fist clench into a ball from the corner of my eye.

"You have no alibi, except for the lie and those who agreed to lie for you," he says.

"I was ill that day, so I didn't go to work. Mother and Father decided to cancel their trip to Allastair's to pay me and Violette a visit. Who else could have confirmed my presence home, but those who saw me there?"

"You were a grown man," Lottie says. "Why would your parents change their plans just because you had a cold?"

"Flu, actually."

"Did you see the doctor?" Patrick asks.

I shake my head.

"So you were so ill you needed mummy and daddy with you, but not ill enough to see the doctor."

I have nothing to say out loud to this. All I can think is that there is a reason our parents never bonded with him, but they did with me.

"I came to the house as soon as I heard about Timothy's disappearance," Patrick resumes. "Your car was there, but no one else's. No one answered the door."

"I was taken to bed, I wouldn't have opened the door even if the police announced themselves."

"*No one else* was in your house, and yet you told the police Mum, Dad, and Violette were."

"They *were*," and I refrained from adding 'you idiot'.

"What about Rebecca's statement?" Alicia says. "Because I never digested that. Where did it come from?"

"She made it up for–"

"Oh quit it, Ellis," she snaps. "We all know Killian and Mum bullied her into retracting everything."

Her tone shocks me. She's been harbouring this feeling for a while, and here I was thinking she'd been neutral this entire time. I suppose the circumstances are bringing true feelings into the open.

"She saw Violette and her father standing outside her house," Alicia continues, "gesturing wildly, and then Violette handing Timothy's cardigan to Killian. That cardigan has been missing ever since. How could Rebecca possibly know this, if she hadn't witnessed it with her own eyes?"

"I don't have an answer to that. All I know is that she admitted making it all up."

Lottie's crying now. Violette is staring at me. I know that look, and it frightens me. Terrifies me. My blood flow comes to a halt.

"I don't want to believe you had anything to do with it," Alicia says with a hardness in her eyes I've never seen before, "but I need answers in order to put it behind me. I suspect it's the same for Patrick and Lottie. And saying Rebecca made everything up just won't cut it."

I can't bring myself to flex a single muscle. Only my eyes are moving in their sockets.

"What's really been bothering me," Patrick says, "is the book you received for Christmas. Why do you think the murderer, a person as evil as one can get, is saying *you* should go to hell? He knows something. Something we don't, or perhaps we do, and just can't act on it. What did you do, Ellis?"

I can only stare at him. Nothing, is the answer. But I've already said that countless times, and they've never accepted it.

"Did you kill Rebecca to make sure she'd never come back on her words?" Patrick goes on.

It takes every effort to move my muscles, but I shake my head, slowly, left and right, with as much difficulty as if I were restrained with ropes.

"Violette," Alicia says, "tell us what you know. What were you doing outside Killian's house with Timothy's cardigan?"

"Keep her out of it," I say, my voice sounding foreign to me. "She was never at Killian's that day."

Alicia doesn't even look in my direction. "Violette?"

Violette is just staring at me. I'm willing her to keep quiet with every fibre of my body – and for now, she does.

"Are you trying to protect her?" Patrick asks me. "What does she need to be protected from?" He takes a deep breath and takes a step towards me. I'm still sitting down at the table, turned towards Violette but not facing Patrick. He's coming at me from the side. "What did you do to my son?" His voice is like a snarl.

Violette's eyes are moist. Every single trait on her face is trembling, as if shaking from cold.

"You weren't ill that day," Patrick goes on with demonic determination. "No one knew where you were, you have no alibi, so you got your wife and mummy to lie for you. Killian was only too happy to see me in pain so he tagged along. You let your burning jealousy get the better of you, and you took what was most precious to me. You always had Mum and Dad's love, you could do nothing wrong, whereas I was the brat who had the wrong interests, the wrong personality, the outcast in my own family, but that wasn't enough for you. When I managed to make it in life *despite* my upbringing and your every effort to keep me in the bottom of the pit, you took everything I did personally, even though I've never given a flying fuck about you. Once I was old enough to get the hell out of Mum's house, I could no longer care less about you and your stupid insecurities. My house, the holiday home, my becoming CEO, *nothing* to do with you. Did you know I offered to buy Mum a house in Italy, to help with her lungs? She got offended, insulted me for my arrogance. I will never understand what I did to you both – I mean, I never took the attention away from you, did I? – but you've always hated me. And you chose to take it out on a defenceless child. Coward doesn't even begin to describe you."

Violette's mouth opens.

"Fine," I say quickly, and stare into his eyes. I watch the slightest sign of pain creep onto his face with rare pleasure. "Fine, Patrick."

At this moment, Julian gestures towards Tilly. Charlie puts an arm around her and takes her into the kitchen.

"Yes," I continue, "I killed your son."

His pupils dilate, but other than that, it looks like his eyes have emptied. A void has formed, and it swallows everything around. The silence is total. No movement, no wind outside, no one is breathing. I certainly am not; I'm holding it in until he says something.

Then he moves, and it all happens very quickly. Before I can even duck or try to tackle him, he's gotten the gun out from behind his back and he fires.

The bullet lodges itself in my left breast, and a flash of pain blinds everything out.

As I collapse over the chairs and then the floor, and just before I sink into the comforting darkness, I hear Violette's high-pitched scream as if from another dimension: "*Non*! It was me!"

And that hurts more than the wound itself.

27

VIOLETTE

I kneel next to my husband and kiss him to try and feel his breath on my face, but there's no point. He's gone. I can barely see through the tears.

Alicia lifts me up and she's in my face, shouting things, but I can't process it. Leon takes over from Alicia, and I gladly fall into my son's arms. After a few moments, when I've recovered some composure, I can only notice the complete silence coming from Patrick and Lottie. They're staring unblinkingly at me.

"You can't just scream that and not elaborate," Alicia says. "In the circumstances, frankly, I do not care if your husband and my brother is dead right now." She gives Patrick a hard look. "We'll deal with that later."

Ellis sacrificed himself for me. The thought brings tears back to my eyes. If only I'd talked earlier, just a few seconds, he'd still be here. How can I be such a coward?

Sacrifice isn't the right word, because I spilled it the moment he was shot. I rendered his death meaningless. I did the worst thing I could possibly have done.

I lift my head and meet Patrick and Lottie's eyes. "He is guilty of protecting the woman he loves, but not of killing the child."

Patrick's expression is lifeless. It's like he's empty on the inside, like his soul left so he could summon up the coldness to kill. Lottie's face is tense, anxious. She's looking at me as if the fate of the world rests on the next word I will say.

"It was an accident." The pain and wrenching desire to convince them I'm telling the truth twist my face. "I swear it was. I just wanted to scare you, to teach you a lesson." Leon lets go of me and takes a step back. "You made Ellis so unhappy; he couldn't bear to see you so different, to see you do so much better than him in life and shove it in his face. All I cared about was for him to be happy, and in that respect, I was powerless. Nothing I could do to erase that pain. He wouldn't act on his threats and it got to me. I thought he may have peace at last if he saw that you had more misfortune than him. And it wasn't hard for me, because...I couldn't stand Lottie's parenting." I look away, at the rug, the table, anywhere but Lottie's direction. I have to convince myself she's not there. "She was soft and negligent and she allowed the boy to grow feral. It all fell into place. The lesson would hit two birds with one stone."

"What did you *do*?" Alicia says, clenching her hands in front of her.

"I thought I was braver than Ellis so I took things into my own hands. I knew Lottie's routine after school. I took him, told him we were going to visit his uncle and cousin. I was just going to keep him for a bit, until the evening perhaps, and return him."

My throat closes as I think of what happened next. I close my eyes, force some saliva down, and push the words out.

"In the car I...he shouted he needed to pee, so I stopped on the side of the road." Lottie's sobbing hysterically now, but I block it off or I will never finish. "We went on the grass, I led him to a bush, and then...then he just bolted off. I grabbed his cardigan but it came away. I ran after him, but the surprise gave him enough of a lead to stay out of my grasp. He ran towards the river, I think he thought he might run across it, or he didn't think about the fact he couldn't swim. Anyway, he tried to stop himself, but he slipped and fell in. I jumped in...the current was strong...I didn't catch him up until it was too late."

I want to say how sorry I am, but I know that is utterly useless. Nothing I can say will ever make it better, save for what I've already said.

Lottie is shaking, spasm after spasm, and it is so incredibly painful to watch. I tense with every convulsion. I expect Patrick to turn to me and shoot, but he's trying to calm Lottie. The darkness which came over him when he killed Ellis is no longer there. Why won't he kill me? I'm resigned to my fate. I fully deserve it. Should've turned myself in all those years ago, but I let Ellis and Norah and Killian convince me to keep quiet. I have no longer anything to live for, with Ellis gone and my crime in the open. If Patrick doesn't kill me, it will be prison for the rest of my life.

Julian tries to hug Alicia but she pushes him away. She's seething. She glares at me, then shakes her head and storms into the kitchen.

"What happened to the cardigan?" Julian asks.

"Killian disposed of it for me. Rebecca's original statement was correct."

Charlie is still in the kitchen with Tilly, and I'm glad I can't see her judging me. Leon, however, has backed away into the corner of the dining room, staring blankly ahead of him. It's like he saw a ghost. The ghost of the mother he knew departing forever.

"Kill me," I tell Patrick.

He ignores me.

"If you don't, I will grab that gun and do it myself."

Lottie emerges from her fit. I flinch. Her eyes are so bloodshot they're verging on brown.

"No," she growls, "you have to suffer. You have to face justice."

She takes a few steps forward and punches me flat on the nose. The blinding pain makes me bend over, and even as I taste the metallic tang of blood, I know this does not come even close to a fraction of the pain I've inflicted her.

28

ALICIA

I couldn't speak or see anyone for some time. I tidied the kitchen, opened and closed cupboard doors without taking anything out or placing anything inside. I couldn't make sense of it, or understand how anyone could be so base and small minded as to take things to such a moronic level. Orchestrate a kidnapping just to teach a lesson? To punish someone for being successful? Was this even possible, or was she covering for the real reason? Something inside told me she was telling the truth, but it made no sense to me. I heard her ask Patrick to kill her, and when Patrick didn't, I considered doing it myself. I'd never been violent before, or even fought the urge to hit someone, but I also had never been faced with this kind of situation.

It definitely took the edge off Mum's passing. She wasn't a saint, and God knows she emotionally abused us until her last breath, but I didn't think she could go this far. I knew the signs were there, the lies too obvious, and in hindsight, it had been staring at me in the face the entire time. But it would have destroyed me – and my life – to understand the truth earlier, and I must have subconsciously protected myself by burying my head in the sand.

The killer was still lurking anonymously, we were all still at risk, and yet I no longer cared. It was like too much danger cancelled itself. My sister-in-law had effectively murdered my nephew, and my brother, both parents, and close cousin had been in on it for almost two decades. What could possibly beat this? My death? No. My children were safe, thousands of miles from here. Julian's death, yes. But I was not in a state to worry about him.

They cleared Ellis' corpse, then Charlie prepared some snacks for a late lunch slash early dinner. I had helped with every meal so far, but not this time. Julian stood in for me and assisted Charlie in cutting up pies and heating some leftovers.

While I was still submerged in this pensive, carefree haze, I heard what happened next like distant noises in the background. Violette said she needed to change and use the bathroom, Leon said he'd go and wait at the bottom of the stairs to ease everyone's anxieties as to leaving someone alone. There was no one else upstairs so she couldn't kill anyone, and if she died somehow...frankly, I was not sure anyone cared.

Then, some time later, Leon shouted down the staircase in a remake of his announcement of Melissa's death. I didn't budge. Patrick and Lottie stayed with me while Julian, Charlie, and Tilly went up to see what the fuss was about.

Violette hanged herself using the rope which had held Rebecca suspended mid-air, in the master bedroom. The only emotion I felt was frustration and indignation. She shouldn't be able to get off the hook so easily. Judging by the look in Lottie's eyes, she felt the same way, but to her credit she didn't say anything. I did feel sympathy for Leon and Charlie, and that's why I didn't say anything either, and asked Julian to move her body outside as soon as he could to save her children the pain of seeing their mother in that state. Patrick volunteered to help Julian move the corpse, and I guessed this was a good way for him to get some closure.

There were now only seven of us left: Patrick, Lottie, Tilly, Charlie, Leon, Julian, and myself. Perhaps Tristan if he was still alive, wherever he was. Someone somewhere was laughing at the purge of the Morrisons. In what, three days? The family had been reduced by more than half. It was almost comical. And well deserved, considering what had just been revealed.

We sat together in the dining room, mostly in silence, lost in our thoughts. The table was empty, save for a half-melted candle and the bottle of whiskey we opened last night. I didn't have any, I hate whiskey. It was next to impossible to believe that the murderer was one of us. I was more and more inclined to believe someone outside our group was responsible, sheltering outside the house and striking unseen. Somehow. It seemed implausible, but the possibility of one of these six people being responsible appeared even more outrageous. Perhaps a partnership? Someone in here working with someone else outside? No, it would still mean someone here was responsible.

"What now?" Julian asked, and it was like a branch had slammed the window. Tilly even jumped at his voice.

"We wait," Leon said.

"What for?" Charlie asked.

"Rescue," Leon replied. "For someone to come. The tenant farmer is bound to come to the barn sooner or later."

Patrick shook his head. "We can't just wait. We still haven't caught the killer. Not to mention we might run out of food soon."

It was my turn to shake my head. "There are plenty of tins in the pantry. And there are fewer and fewer of us."

"What about water?" Charlie asked.

"Fine too," I said. "The house is gravity fed by a surface well."

"What if we follow the electric line across fields?" Charlie suggested. "We might encounter a house or commercial building that is closer than we knew?"

"The house is not on mains electrics," Patrick said. "Too remote. The power comes from a turbine in the river. But I do think walking away from here is the only way we'll get out. It's a long walk, but people have walked further before. We can take food with us, the right equipment."

"We don't have tents," Julian points out.

"Yes, that's an issue."

"In winter," Julian goes on. "We won't make it past the first night."

"But we may not make it past another night here either."

"We need to make a bonfire," Leon said, "throw some tyres in it. It will create a plume of black smoke, and someone will see it and understand it's a call for help."

"Nobody saw the huge cloud of black smoke following the petrol explosion," Patrick pointed out, and I closed my eyes as the memory of Flynn and Kacey surfaced.

"Maybe nobody happened to see it at the time," Leon said, "but it doesn't mean no one will if we create another one today."

A moment of silence.

"I think that's the best thing we can do right now," Charlie said.

"Me too," Lottie agreed.

Patrick paused, then nodded. "I don't have a better suggestion."

"I'll get the lighter from the kitchen," I said, and Charlie stood up to get the firelighters from the fireplace.

Having a sensible plan gave us energy, and it enabled me to put the recent events in the back of my mind for now. I opened the cutlery drawer and over the cutlery tray lay a folded sheet of paper. It had not been there earlier, while I was idly tidying, so I knew it had been planted there by the killer. I froze; I did not want to unfold it and discover what it said. The last time we'd done this, two people had ended up dead.

It had also solved a lifelong mystery, though.

How could I not look? The burning curiosity was irresistible. Were there any other secrets to unravel? I couldn't think of any.

I glanced behind me; Julian was throwing something into the bin, but other than him, no one else was in the kitchen with us. I took the note and unfolded it.

∾

AT FIRST, I had no idea what I was looking at. Numbers and lines and charts. I had been expecting clear, self-explanatory text, like the previous note, but this was a messy jumble of characters. Then I spotted my name above a set of lines and numbers, and on the opposite side, on a different set of lines, was the name *Timothy Morrison*. My eyes scanned the rest of the document, and rested on the bottom of the page. *Conclusion: 0% (No relation)*.

My eyes flew to the top of the page, and my heart dropped in my chest. *DNA Test*.

I felt a presence behind me and tensed. I risked a glance over my shoulder, my pulse racing. It was Julian.

"What is this?" he asked.

I gave him the document. The blood flow pounded in my ears.

"Everything okay?" Came Leon's voice, and it didn't take long before everybody else joined us in the kitchen.

I watched Lottie and Patrick with trepidation as they read it. They both turned to me in unison. Same for Leon. Was it accusation I saw in their eyes? Why was no one looking at Lottie?

"What does it mean?" Charlie asked.

"It means," Julian said, "that Timothy and Alicia aren't related. So either Alicia is not Norah's biological daughter, and therefore doesn't share any DNA with Patrick. Or..."

"Or Patrick wasn't his biological father, rather," I hastened to say. It hadn't even come to my mind that I might not be Mum's biological child. That was ridiculous; I looked like Dad and Ellis, no one could ever doubt my origins.

"Or Patrick is the one who was adopted," Lottie added. "But anyway, what is this?" She pointed derogatively at the sheet of paper. "It came from the killer, right? So he likely doctored it to say what he wants it to say. He wants us to kill each other, and so far it has worked beautifully for him."

"I don't know," Patrick said, "so far it seems to me the killer has not lied with the information he's revealed. I don't know how he knows these things, but he does. And if this test is genuine... How did he make it happen?" His eyes fall on me. "Maybe it's not a *he* after all. How else would the killer have gotten a sample of your DNA?"

A hot wave of outrage rises in me, but I do my best to keep it down. Is he truly suspecting *me*? "I don't know. Julian?"

Patrick's eyes widen. "Are you saying your husband is behind all this?"

"No, no, but we're all family, it's the easiest thing to get a sample of my DNA. What about getting Timothy's DNA? That's the most difficult bit. Would've been easiest for you to do that. Do you really think I'd be so dumb as to put this out with my name on it if I were the killer?"

He shrugged. "Nothing can be left out."

"What about the possibility that you're not the father?" I said, then turned to Lottie. I regretted putting her in that position instantly, but in my defence, I was flustered by Patrick's suggestion.

"Hold on a second," Charlie said, her gaze going blank. "The book you got on Christmas Eve, Patrick, it was the Poldark book, right? Warleggan. I watched the series, and when Julian and Alicia recalled what happened in that book, I remembered that season. It was the best one. It wasn't just Francis' death, the main event was Ross cheating on Demelza."

"That's right," Julian said, nodding. "Warleggan was the cuckold. And then Demelza almost cheated on Ross with that Scottish captain."

"So cheating was definitely one of that book's main themes," Charlie added. "It's probably where the killer is going with this. Whether it's true or not…"

"Of course it's not!" shouted Lottie. "Don't be ridiculous."

Patrick shook his head without speaking at first, then said, "No, I don't think she did. We were happy then."

"Absolutely ludicrous to even suggest it," Lottie went on, waving her hands.

"What is that?" Julian asked, his attention directed at something behind me. He strode across the kitchen, and just before he snatched it, I saw it was another sheet of paper sticking out from behind the framed painting of a stormy beach on the wall.

"Oh my goodness," I said, "will it ever end?"

Julian remained speechless when he finished reading, and he let the document float to the ground, as if frozen in space. Leon precipitated himself onto the letter, and allowed the other three to read along with him. Only Tilly and I didn't rush over. I didn't think I could stomach more devastating news, more revelations which would lead to more death. I didn't want to read it.

Charlie sucked air through her teeth.

Leon muttered something I couldn't hear.

Patrick stared at Lottie.

Lottie stared at Julian.

Julian was still staring at his clenched hand.

29

JULIAN

Two years before Timothy's death

He stood in font of his car, the envelope in his hands, his gaze fixed on Lottie's letter box in front of him. If he walked over and slid the letter inside, his life would likely change for good. What if Patrick found the letter first, and opened it? It was a significant risk, but he couldn't have this conversation with Lottie in person, not after the way she'd been behaving ever since that day.

The front door opened, and Lottie appeared in the doorway. She waved him over. She wore a light floral dress, appropriate for this warm Spring day, and it suited her to a tee. No wonder he'd caved in when the opportunity had presented itself.

She leaned against the doorframe and looked enquiringly at him.

He had to think on his feet; he couldn't tell her the real reason for his presence. "Cameron's birthday party," he said, fiddling with the envelope in his hands. "Just wanted to pass on the invitation to you and Timothy."

She gave him a sideways smile. "A bit early, isn't it?"

He peeked inside the house. "A bit quiet for a Thursday morning. Is Timothy napping?"

"He's trialling the nursery up the road. I have my first morning to myself in a long time."

He knew this was the best time to mention it, he'd never have a better opportunity, but it could go horribly wrong. Never mind, he needed to get it off his chest.

"Do you think I could spend some time with Timothy, when convenient for you?"

She frowned, confused. "Just the two of you?"

He nodded.

"Why? That would be odd, wouldn't it? Maybe when he's older. You're his uncle, I suppose you could do some sort of activity together."

He thought about the letter in his hands. Should he just hand it over and leave? "Listen," he said, staring at the envelope, "we never talked about the timing of our...hiccup."

She stopped him instantly. "No." She shook her head vehemently. "No no no no. You shut your mouth. There is no doubt whatever that Patrick is his father. Biological or else, and don't you dare suggest otherwise. Do you hear me?" He stared at her in silence. "Julian, do you *hear* me?"

There was fire in her eyes, the kind of which he'd never seen before.

He nodded, then folded the envelope and tucked it in his coat's inside pocket.

30

JULIAN

Leon walks towards Alicia, the document in his hand. Lottie plants herself firmly in front of him, blocking his way.

Julian risks a glance at Lottie; every inch of her face is trembling. Her eyes tell Leon not to do this, and Leon meets her gaze with the same fierceness. He steps around Lottie, but she grabs his arm. "Please," she says, "don't. It will destroy her. I've never seen this letter before."

Leon doesn't say a word. Julian wonders what Patrick is doing right now. How has he not said something yet, or taken his revolver out? That's why he has remained frozen in space; he doesn't dare meet Patrick's eyes. He expects hands to wrap around his throat at any moment. It's not like his brother-in-law has shown total self-control today.

And then there's Alicia.

Leon snatches his arm away from Lottie's grasp and hands the letter to Alicia.

Julian can hear the words as his wife reads them. His apology for turning Lottie's life upside down. The results of the DNA test he performed. His pledge to provide regular payments for the child, if she wants him to. His promise that he will never, ever, mention it to anyone else, let alone Patrick. His agreement that it was a mistake, and they should just put it behind them.

The first thing Alicia does is look up from the letter and fix her eyes on Julian. He doesn't look directly at her. He can feel the pressure of her stare from the corner of his eye. He's holding his breath, and no one else is saying anything.

Without a word to him, she slowly turns to Lottie. "You never saw this letter before, you said. But do you deny what it says? Proves, even. I recognise my husband's handwriting."

Lottie risks a glance at Patrick, then melts into a puddle of tears. It's hard to tell if she's trying to say something or not.

"Julian?" His wife says in a lifeless voice.

He slowly meets her eyes, and sees decades of their lives crumble to dust. Their bond is permanently broken, no matter what he does now. He never thought he'd see this brokenness in his wife's eyes, let alone directed at him. All the good times they spent, the things they created together, the life that was theirs, he can almost see it all vaporise into thin air.

And she doesn't even know everything yet.

Patrick's voice puts an end to the moment. "Is it true, Charlotte? Was Timothy not my son?"

He clearly has no care for the fact she can barely hold herself upright. The tears are streaming down her cheeks, sticky saliva drooling out of the corner of her lips, and all Julian can think of is Tilly. She shouldn't see her parents in this state, she shouldn't have to witness any of this. Charlie is trying to get her to look away, she's embracing her, but she's still watching over Charlie's shoulder.

Lottie manages to mouth some intelligible words amid her blubbering. "I truly don't think he's the father. But...a moment of anxiety, just one moment when we decided to try for children. I– I– I started questioning whether I wanted to be with you for the rest of my life, and– and Julian was there." Patrick moves and she flinches. "I'm so, so, so sorry."

Now Julian feels the need to explain. "As the letter says, it was a huge mistake. We both regretted instantly, and thought it would create more damage to say anything than to forget about it. And I think it was the right decision." He turns to Alicia. "We had a good life, didn't we? It would have ruined everything."

And there it is, at last. The metallic click as the gun is cocked.

Julian turns back around and the weapon is pointed at him. Patrick has the same look in his eyes he had when he pulled the trigger on Ellis. A black stare, devoid of emotions. Like a hitman performing routine work. No tears, no furrowed brow. His lips form a flat line, and his eyelids are verging on droopy.

"No," Leon says, "not again. What will it solve? We've seen enough deaths, Patrick."

But his words hit a twice reinforced concrete wall and fall flat at its feet.

"Not in front of your daughter," Leon tries again, and it's like Charlie wakes up. She drags Tilly away from the kitchen and into the hallway. "Are you the killer?" Leon resumes. "Did you orchestrate all this in order to get back at the people who killed your son? And to exact your revenge on the real father, which you knew all along?"

Julian sees a way to save his skin. "And why, of everyone here, are both your wife and daughter still alive? A bit of a coincidence, isn't it?"

"And when you found the gun," Leon says, "by the well, I checked that you weren't the killer, remember? You never gave me an answer."

Charlie appears in the doorway, without Tilly. "You're the one who saw Melissa and me, aren't you? At the dinner after that, you said that people under stress have odd impulses, and you were staring at Melissa while you said it." She disappears to return by Tilly's side.

Silence follows, during which only Lottie's sniffles can be heard. Julian expected Patrick to react to these accusations, for it to get into his head and extricate him from his murderous frame of mind.

But the emptiness is still there. It's like he heard nothing of what was just thrown at him.

"Violette killed Timothy," Patrick says at last, staring unblinkingly at Julian, his voice monotone and deep. "But you took the memory of my son away from me."

Julian expects the gunshot to ring out, but nothing comes. He realises just now how utterly silent Alicia has been. Why didn't she explode, call him all manner of names? Why isn't she stopping her brother from killing her husband? He wants to turn to her, but he doesn't dare look away from the gun.

"Alicia," Patrick says, "if you want me to stop, say the word."

Julian turns to his wife, hopeful. Patrick is giving him a chance, which is more than Ellis got.

But Alicia merely stares at her husband, with a lifeless energy oddly similar to her brother's. Her lips part, ever so slightly, but nothing comes out.

Patrick takes a step forward. Perhaps to remove any chance of missing his target.

"I don't care if he kills me," Julian tells Alicia. "Just say *something*!"

He is terrified of dying without hearing his wife's reaction.

She stares at him as if he's a stranger. He can't bring himself to understand what must be going on in her mind. Does she not want to talk it out? Has she truly given up on him so quickly? So much so that she is willing to see him die in front of her? What about the past forty years...*forty* years! Gone in a fleeting moment.

"The next step I take," Patrick says, "I pull the trigger."

"Alicia, please, speak!"

A second goes by, and still nothing. Patrick steps forward.

The gun goes off.

Julian crashes to the floor, the bullet lodged deeply into his left breast. Like Ellis.

Patrick leaves the room without waiting to see if he'll die. Lottie runs to Julian, but Alicia shoves her aside and she falls hard on the tiled floor.

As he twists in pain in his own blood, Julian glimpses Charlie's head pop in to see what happened. He gathers all his strength and says, looking at his niece: "The mother's milk is toxic. Lethal."

He has no doubt they all think he's delirious.

Lottie scrambles back up and leaves the kitchen. Leon follows her out, and takes Charlie with him. Alicia walks over and crouches next to Julian. They are alone in the room.

The pain is ripping through his chest, travelling all over his body. A numbness starts forming in his toes and fingers. He wills it to grow quicker in order to suppress the atrocious pain.

Alicia places her elbows on her knees, hands flapping in the middle. As if bending down to give him a pep talk. He wants to raise himself up and straighten his head to look her level in the eye, but his body no longer obeys him. He's stuck with his face on the cold tiled floor, mouth open.

"I didn't let Patrick shoot because you cheated on me twenty years ago," she says. "That in itself might have been reason enough – God knows you've been a real shit for lying all these years – but no, we may have been able to work through it, for the sake of our boys, for the sake of peace in our retirement."

Her eyes are hard, her mouth harder. Where has his wife gone?

"I let him shoot and now I regret it. I think it was a kindness. We should have made you pay. *Really* pay."

He tries to ask what she means, but only slurred noises come out.

"I know, Julian." A tear forms in her left eye. A tear born of anger. "You're the sick fuck behind this massacre." She wipes her nose with the back of her hand. The words struggle to come out. "I know, because I know you better than anyone else. I started having some doubts when we understood the books had meaning. But all along I didn't truly believe it could be you. I was in denial, obviously. How could I not be? My husband who I met when I was still a girl, who has been by my side my entire life, the father of my children. How could he be the author of such atrocities? But when I read this letter, it hit me. The reality of it forced my eyes open. You've been a conniving fuck since the beginning."

It doesn't matter that he can't speak or move, because he would have been paralysed anyway. How has she found out? He has been so careful. She must have read his puzzlement in his eyes, for she says:

"The choice of books on Christmas Eve was you down to the marrow. Game of Thrones? Poldark? Crime and Punishment? The

Great Gatsby, for God's sake. All your favourite books. Who else has read all these books and knows them enough to use as messages? No one in this family, that's for sure. But when you planted a reference to Dante's *Inferno* under Melissa's corpse, in addition to giving the actual book to Ellis, it slapped me in the face. Yet still, I refused to acknowledge it.

"And then there was your 'alibi'. When you left for your work convention just before Christmas, something felt off. You went to the same convention last year, in Brighton too, yet last year you took a cab to go to the airport because it didn't make sense to drive and pay for parking. And I've never known you to drive to the airport. You either get dropped off, or you catch a cab. But this year you took the car. Now I understand why. You drove in the opposite direction. I don't know how you got that receipt with the convenient date to exonerate you, but I know you're clever enough to fake it."

The numbness has taken over his limbs. He's becoming heavier and heavier, as if he's sinking into the tiles. The fatigue is overwhelming. His vision is starting to go, along with his awareness.

"They may not know you well enough to have noticed," she goes on, "but not once did you show a moment of anxiety, or fear, for what might happen to you. Or me. The fact that there was a killer around us, amongst us, didn't seem to affect you whatsoever. You were totally indifferent. You have a brain for riddles, you love them, and when we were looking for the can of petrol, you barely spoke. How could I not take note of that?"

The disgust on her face pains him. He never wanted to ruin what they had, though he knew it would happen sooner or later. He no longer wants to be there. The darkness can't come soon enough.

"I'm not going to claim I know why you did it, and frankly I don't care. Nothing can justify this. And any explanation will just make me angrier. But when I learned about you and Lottie, and how you'd kept it from me all these years, and how calculating you can be, it all made sense. You're a master at lying. You always were passionate about Timothy's murder, and of course you should be, even to my eyes you were his uncle, but you never cared much about your other nephews and nieces. I don't think you've ever spent any time alone with Tilly or Charlie or Leon in your life. It all came together then."

She rakes her nose and throat, and spits on him. The glob lands on his cheekbone.

"Kacey?" Her eyes are about to burst. "Melissa? Flynn? And what about Tilly? You've ruined her life. Tristan too, the poor innocent soul who found himself in your version of hell. If he's still alive. How could you?"

She stands up, and lifts her foot as if about to kick his face, but seems to think better of it.

She leaves the room, closes the door, flicks the switch, and plunges him into darkness.

31

LOTTIE

The moment I enter the dining room, I rush to Patrick's side. "Patrick, please." I sniff loudly as I feel the phlegm creep onto my upper lip. "Say something."

I'm a mess. My face is wet and hot and cold all at once. A voice inside my head tells me to pull it together, but I can't control the spasming and the tears. In front of me stands the man of my life, the only man I've ever loved, and he is slipping away from me.

"You are and always have been his father, no matter what a stupid test says."

I grab his arm but he shakes me off. He's staring out of the window, the grey light falling unevenly on his face. If only he could say something, to give me an idea of what is tormenting him the most.

"Julian means nothing to me, he never has! It's just... I had that miscarriage, do you remember? I felt the loss so deeply, and I felt so alone. I'm not blaming you for anything, but you didn't seem to understand my pain, and there was no one I could talk to. One time, just one time, Julian came to our flat when you were out, I don't remember why, and he listened. It was stupid and I have regretted it every second for the rest of my life, but it does not mean my love for you ever wavered. It meant absolutely nothing."

Patrick growls something I don't catch.

"What was that?" I ask. "Please say it again."

"It meant everything," he mutters. "Is Tilly mine?"

I gape at him, utterly shocked. "Of course, how..." But I know exactly how he can doubt it. I made the greatest mistake and it is costing me everything.

For a moment, I wonder if Tilly is in the room and listening to this. I have no awareness beyond Patrick and his window. The deaths seem so trivial; my own survival holds no importance to me right now. I don't know who the psychopath is, and I don't care. My soul is dying.

"I didn't say anything because it would have ruined your life," I resume. "And because it meant nothing *to me*. If it had been about something deeper, then I would have come clean. But it *wasn't*. It was just a fleeting moment of weakness, with the worst timing possible. It was the same for Julian, so it would've been madness to ruin so many people's lives for a huge, but foolish mistake."

I get nothing from him. His eyes do not flicker, his nervous twitch of the cheek is absent. As if he's blocking me out completely. The gun is held loosely in his left hand, and at this point I would prefer it if he directed it at me. God knows I deserve it. I failed the most important people in my life: my son and my husband.

I hear steps coming into the room and snap out of it.

I need a drink.

32

CHARLIE

Lottie poured herself a generous dose of whiskey. Then she remembered there were other people in the room, and offered the bottle to Leon. He filled his glass to the brim and then served me a measure. I thought he may offer some to Tilly too, given the circumstances, but it seemed her age still refrained him from doing so.

He ignored Patrick, but he was out of it anyway. He didn't even seem to hear anything we were saying. He merely stared out of the window, the gun still in his hand. That made me uncomfortable, but I wasn't about to voice it now.

Alicia returned into the dining room, and all heads turned in her direction. Her cheeks were wet, but I couldn't see any sadness on her face. Or grief. If anything, she seemed cross. Disgusted even, perhaps. She didn't say anything, and none of us dared ask. Patrick may not have noticed she'd even come in; he was still staring outside.

"Whiskey?" Leon offered, lifting the bottle up.

She took a moment before looking in his direction. "No, no, I don't drink that. Don't like it."

I expected her to keep on talking, but she just walked to the table and gently laid her hands on the back of a chair. Leon downed his glass, while Lottie sipped on hers. The tension was too high for me to bring the glass to my lips. Was Julian dead? Was Patrick responsible for it all? Wasn't anyone going to address it?

"We're safe," Alicia said at last. "The killer, he's gone."

"Actually," Leon said with a glint in his eye which told me he may have already had some whiskey before I came into the room, "he's not. He's right there." He pointed to Patrick. "With a loaded gun in his hand, I may add. Is–" He brought a hand to his chest, and frowned.

"No," Alicia said, "it was Julian. He... It's all his doing. And he's dead now, so the danger has gone. I should have seen it sooner, and for that I apologise."

Something clicked inside me, and his last words suddenly made sense. The mother's milk... If he was the killer, then in an odd change of heart, he was warning me!

I dropped the glass and let it shatter on the floor. Then I lunged for the bottle of whiskey and smashed it against the wall. I grabbed Lottie's glass and threw it too, but feared it may have been too late; her glass was almost empty.

By the time I turned to Leon he was on the floor, his hands wrapped around his throat.

"He's poisoned it," I said.

All the noise got Patrick to leave the window, but he still didn't seem to register.

I looked at Leon twist on the floor, the glass shards cutting into his skin, and knew there was nothing I or anyone could do.

"Mum," Tilly said, coming up to Lottie. "Are you– How are you feeling?"

Lottie shook her head. "My throat is closing." Terror was carved across her face. Tilly's mouth contorted, her hands clenched mid-air, paralysed by fear.

"So Karma has a name," Patrick said. He looked at me with a slightly hysterical smile. "Julian."

The unbearable feeling of powerlessness will stay with me until I give my last breath. There my aunt was, a woman I loved as a friend and a second mother, dying a painful death in front of my eyes, the pain doubled by her daughter's presence, and there was not a single thing I could do. I clenched my fists so hard my nails dug into the flesh, and to this day I still have the scars.

Patrick watched her die with a cold heart.

Mine was forever mutilated.

∼

WE COULDN'T BRING ourselves to move the corpses. We cleaned the dining room of the glass and poisoned whiskey, covered the bodies with blankets, and closed the dining room's two doors, never intending to go back in there ever again.

Patrick had been in the sitting room all along, and we joined him there. He was standing behind the sofa. When he turned to us, it appeared as though he'd finally awoken. There was an alertness in his eyes which had been missing earlier.

"I know I'm done," he said. "Julian may be responsible for all this, but I killed my brother and brother-in-law. There are witnesses. I'll die behind bars."

He brought the gun to his head. Alicia screamed and ran to him, but he pointed the weapon immediately at her, and she stopped in her tracks.

"Back off, or I *will* shoot."

No one could take his threats lightly anymore. Alicia took a few steps back, until the sofa was between them again.

He brought the gun back to his temple. "What will you tell the police, if we ever get out?" he asked Alicia.

"The truth," she replied. "That I married a psychopath and he's responsible for everything."

"What about Ellis and Julian?"

"I'll tell them the truth, Patrick. You have nothing to worry about, truly. He manipulated us, threatened us with our lives. Killing him was an act of self-defence."

His eyes flickered. "But I killed *Julian* for what he did to me twenty years ago, not the killer for what he did these past few days. In any justice system, I'm a murderer. Two-time murderer."

Alicia didn't reply to this, because there was nothing to say.

He turned to his daughter. "I'm sorry, Tilly. I really am. I wish you hadn't been here, but you are, and there's no going back now. I can never recover from this. It's just...too much. I spent twenty years, your entire life..." He rubbed his eyes with his free hand. "You won't need a father who's serving the rest of his life in prison. You deserve better than me. You need to grow from this, to heal, without the past holding you back."

She hadn't said a word since her mother's death, and she didn't start now. She was in a state of constant weeping, and it only intensified when her father put the gun to his head. I went over and took her in my arms.

"Don't you do this, you fool," Alicia said.

Patrick turned to her. "I appreciate everything you've ever done for me, big sister. The way you've supported me when times were hard, and I understand why you always tried to be neutral when you could, why you tried to avoid conflict, to be the mediator. I would've done the same, had I not been the target of all their resentment. But I only ever felt love and affection coming from you, and you are the best sister I could have asked for. You're a wonderful person, in every aspect, and I suppose the only mistake you ever made was marrying that man."

"Don't you dare say goodbye to me," she muttered through clenched teeth.

His lips didn't smile, but his eyes did. A sad smile, loaded with affection.

Then he turned to me, and I became nervous. Not out of fear, but out of awkwardness. We'd never been close, mainly because my father was Ellis, so I didn't want him to feel like he needed to tell me something just because I was in the room.

"Charlie," he said, "be the big sister Tilly never had, will you? She'll need you. Even if we never got to know each other well, I've always harboured a fondness for you. Continue being you, regardless of what other people say, or think. You're perfect as you are."

My eyes had gotten used, at last, to being dry, but they moistened in an instant and a ball of emotion rose in my throat. I couldn't remember anyone ever telling me this. Why did it have to come from a man who was about to leave us for good?

"Don't," I said. I couldn't help it. It wasn't fair. "Don't go. Stay for her."

The cloud which had glazed his eyes before returned. The hand holding the gun dropped to his side, and for a second I thought he had changed his mind, but he turned around and walked to the door leading to the entrance. Before placing his hand on the handle, he turned to his daughter.

"I love you, Tilly."

Then he went out. Tilly screamed on my chest.

We heard the front door shut, and a few seconds later, a gunshot outside.

I was suddenly acutely aware of the three of us. The survivors.

All the graves were filled, and somehow, Julian had calculated right.

∽

On New Year's Eve, in the morning, a pair of officers from the local police station knocked on the door. We thought it was Tristan at first, or another bad surprise, but when I opened the door, I almost collapsed. I couldn't believe we would actually get out of there alive.

The officers had received an email earlier that morning, mentioning several crimes at this address. They'd believed it to be a prank, a bad joke, but thought they'd check anyway.

They had the shock of their lives when they learned what happened.

As a team searched the house, they found a journal in Julian's name.

33

FINAL LETTER

21 December 2019

I write this before heading to the Morrisons' ancestral home, up in the highlands, to begin my last adventure.

I owe an explanation to the survivors. I hope there will be some. And I suppose there is a hint of vanity in me who wants the world to know how I pulled this off. And if I haven't managed to pull it off...well, I will look a fool. So be it.

I met Alicia when I was twenty. She is my university sweetheart, if there is such a thing. This means I have been in the family a long time, and I've had more than enough time to know the Morrisons through and through. I've come to know all the family secrets, even those unknown to my wife. Secrets which, I hope, will justify my actions. If not justify, at least I hope they will help you understand why I did it.

Alas, the Morrisons' wickedness is not the only reason. It is merely an opportunity, a moral justification, a means to an end. My own wickedness is to blame. I love my wife more than anything; I hope she knows that, even after she learns of my wrongdoings. This love led me to perform unforgivable deeds. I could never say no to her, and wanted to give her the best in everything. My guilt was a dominating factor here, and I was clearly overcompensating, but I'll come to that later. I earned an excellent living as a paediatric surgeon, but Alicia being a housewife and having expensive taste, even a surgeon's salary could not cover our lifestyle's expenses. I wanted that lifestyle too, and I apologise if I made it sound like it was all my wife's fault; it wasn't. In fact, she was always more restrained than I was. She was never one for luxury products and wealth-advertising accessories, whereas I own a Rolex. I could have told her we couldn't afford the house, the travels, the five star hotels, the holiday home. I could have sent the boys to university in London, as opposed to the United States, where a single year – including *all* expenses – could cost one student up to what I make as a surgeon in a year, after taxes. And that was not the Ivy League, either. No, I allowed it, I *wanted* it. I wanted the best for my sons, for my wife, and for myself.

And if I were to offer them the best, I needed the funds. I started taking out personal loans, but I quickly realised that wouldn't cut it. I needed to get my hands on interest-free money, without giving more of my already-scarce free time. An opportunity presented itself at my hospital, and I seized it. I often regretted it afterwards, but once I had started, I could not go back. Organ trafficking served my family and I well over the years, until it caught up to me.

Fast forward a couple of decades, up to last week, when my 'business' partner informed me a law enforcement unit was investigating the hospital, and if I didn't leave now, and forge a new identity and life, I would get caught. I'm sixty years old, only a few years away from retirement. My family has no idea about my illegal activities. I am not going to upturn everything, leave the city I've lived in my entire life, explain to my wife and children why we have to change our names etc etc. It is time to face the consequences of my actions.

However, if I turn myself in, I know I will likely die in prison. I am not willing to do this. So I decided to end it my way, with nothing to lose, and make the Morrisons pay in the process. When my sons announced they would be spending the holidays abroad, I knew Christmas would be the perfect opportunity. Unhoped for, really. All the culprits gathered at the same time, in one of the most secluded and remote spots in the country? Hallelujah.

One does not attempt to exterminate a family without the perfect mix of reasons, and another factor was my crippling guilt. Twenty years ago, I was burdened with debt, we had a young child with mounting expenses, I'd never been so tense and stressed in my life, and long shifts meant I was physically exhausted. Lottie had her own reasons for being in a vulnerable place, and while Patrick and Alicia were out doing sibling stuff, we had intercourse. We instantly regretted, but shortly after that she became pregnant, and I always suspected I may be the father. She wouldn't talk about it with me, so when Timothy was two, I surreptitiously collected some of his DNA and did a test. I was the father. The knowledge effectively ruined my life. I felt like my mistake made me the worst person alive, and anything I could do from then on could not make it worse. I chose to embrace that. If I were to be an asshole, I might as well be financially better off.

This guilt weighed on me every second of every day, it's haunted me, made me sick. I've always hated the family for its toxicity, and I hated myself even more for my part in it. I can no longer bear the guilt. I want to end it. Over the course of the next few days, I will reveal to Alicia and anyone else still standing what I have done.

I wouldn't do what I am about to do if I didn't derive some form of pleasure from inflicting pain on others. As a boy, I always enjoyed making pets and insects suffer, and then killing them. I remember this trap I once set in the woods by my childhood home. It was a snare, and I arrived just before the rabbit would have otherwise died. Oh, the hours of fun I had.

I always hid this side of me, for obvious reasons. I suppose my sense of survival was stronger, my need to be accepted by society more dominant. Society is designed to suppress people like me. If not legally, then personally. If people sense my emptiness, my inclination towards sadism, then they will shun me. But now that I no longer have anything to lose... I'll go ahead and venture that the reason why I've committed crimes must partly come from that frustration, this repression of my own self. It had to come out somehow. And this... experiment...is my last gift to myself. The ultimate feast.

The final unleashing of the wolf amid the sheep.

Now to the Morrisons' sins.

Eleven years ago, Ellis effectively confessed to Timothy's murder in the very house I am heading to. Not to me, naturally, but to Killian. They were in the dining room, and I was in the kitchen. I'd come down in the early night for a glass of water, and they had stayed up drinking after dinner. The door from the kitchen to the dining room was open, and I guess they didn't hear me coming down. Killian was pressing him, trying to provoke him into revealing what truly happened that day. And Ellis admitted at last that, yes, he had made Patrick pay, and the price had to be what was dearest to him. He didn't provide any details, I sensed he was just trying to shut Killian up, but were details necessary?

That confession marked me forever, and I knew that one day or another I'd take care of Ellis, but Killian... He wasn't trying to get to the truth of the matter to obtain justice for Timothy. He wasn't after catching the killer to turn him in, or accusing Ellis of any wrongdoing, or reproaching him in any way. He was *praising* him. Along the lines of, 'Patrick needed to be taken down a peg, I would never have had the guts to do something like that, but boy do I admire the person who did. It was you, wasn't it? Go on cuz, tell me true.' Can you believe it?

Now imagine a family where a mother breaks the law in order to protect her son for the most despicable of crimes, at the expense of her other son, and where the innocent victim is her own four year-old grandchild. A family where the cousin praises his cousin for murdering an innocent child, saying it was well deserved, and who rejoices in his other cousin's despair and crippling grief. A family where that cousin's daughter is a key witness, but is bullied so strongly by her own father and great-aunt that she retracts her story and shuts up forever on the matter.

I'm not the most empathetic of men, but that crossed the line for me. Add to this the fact that the victim is my own flesh, and how could I not exact retribution?

Now to the mechanics of said retribution. I know Norah is planning to go to the house tomorrow, on December twenty-second, so I will join her there. Nobody else is meant to arrive before the twenty-fourth, which gives me twenty-four to thirty-six hours to prepare everything. I told Alicia I need to attend the same convention I attended last year, which took place over the twenty-second and twenty-third, so I must return home on the twenty-third and go back to the highlands on the twenty-fourth with Alicia. I kept a lunch receipt from last year, so I scanned it, photoshopped the year, and printed it back on receipt paper. If anyone asks, I hope this will serve as enough proof.

I will abduct Norah, keep her bound and blind in her car, and hide the car somewhere on the estate. I'm still uncomfortable about killing her, and this will be torture enough to start with, so we'll see how it goes. I plan to record what I have to say and use an app on my phone to modify the voice, so she can't recognise me. I will wear someone else's clothes, so the scent is different. And I will touch her as little as possible, to keep her in doubt whether the abductor is a man or woman. With her out of the way, I will set everything up. The can of petrol, the wires linking the bee hive to the well, the mechanism to make it catch fire if they find the gun first, or drop the ammunition into the well if they find the petrol first. That will take the most time. Hide the poison in the house so I have easy and discreet access. Set up the rope and wire on the master bedroom's ceiling, wrap the books, dig the graves. I hope I've allowed myself enough time. I will empty the tanks of petrol during the first night.

I calculated that it will take less time to reach the gun than it will the can of petrol, and my plan hinges quite heavily on the explosion and someone having a gun. However if it doesn't work out that way, that's fine, I'll adapt. I imagine I'll have to do quite a bit of adapting and improvising. If they find the petrol first, it won't help them escape as I plan to puncture all the cars' petrol tanks beforehand.

As for the books, I've had a lot of fun with that. I wonder if it will occur to them that there is a special meaning to them. It will if they open some of them and see my alterations, but they may not open them until much later. I gave Leon *A Christmas Carol* because I always saw him as Bob Cratchit; I've always been fond of him. I even warned him not to come this year. He is my brightest hope that the Morrison family isn't rotten to the core.

I gave Violette *Les Misérables*, and made it clear on the inside that I was referring to the Thénardier couple. Can you imagine a more perfect reflection in real life? A wife fighting tooth and nail to protect her child murderer of a husband.

I've never read the book I'm giving Norah, but I stumbled upon the review of a film it was adapted from, and couldn't believe the accuracy of the parallels between both mothers. I thought the demise of King Joffrey in *A Song of Ice and Fire* perfect as a foreshadowing of the fate I plan for Killian. I don't know when exactly I'll be able to poison him, but poison is my weapon of choice for him. A painful one. I would hang him on the barbed wire, but he's too heavy. *Robinson Crusoe* for Alicia is an allusion to my hope to see her survive. My plan is for Alicia, Tilly, and Leon to come out alive. I have nothing against Kacey, Melissa, Flynn, Patrick, and Lottie. I would never put their lives in danger in any other context, but unexpected incidents will almost certainly reach them. I will do everything in my power to spare Alicia, Tilly, and Leon, but I'm not super human, and therefore will focus my attentions only on them. Not to mention I may not be able to do anything to protect Patrick and Lottie when emotions run high, even if I want to.

Crime and Punishment for myself, for obvious reasons. Being rattled by guilt for past crimes is the story of my adult life. As for Dante's *Inferno* – and I plan to insert further references to this masterpiece throughout the trip – well, who better to orchestrate a reflection of hell, than Satan himself?

And finally, I scheduled an email to be automatically sent to the closest police station on the thirty-first of December. I've written to Billy, the tenant farmer who farms the estate, to warn him we are grieving significant family losses (we truly will be soon enough) and to please give us some privacy for at least a week. Signed the letter with Ellis' name. So there shouldn't be any intrusions or unexpected rescuers before the email goes out. Fingers crossed.

Alicia, Cameron, Edward, I love you.

And I'm sorry.

Julian

34

MID-TRIP UPDATES

I'm writing this as Alicia is in the bathroom, getting ready for bed. The riddle episode both went according to plan and it didn't. I misjudged many people; I thought Patrick would go for the can of petrol, Ellis for the gun, Leon for the petrol. In the end the gun was found first and the explosion dealt casualties, which was my hope, but the casualties weren't the right ones. Flynn surprised me on this trip. He reacted to his father's death in a very mature way, and I thought he was the type to look after himself and no one else. Yet he went all in for the can of petrol, and when he volunteered to fetch it himself, I had a pang in my heart. I'm kicking myself for not seeing him, for being blinded by his teenager's arrogance. After all, I didn't really know him, I've never spent much time with him. Had I had the time and opportunity, I would've ensured he survived, at least longer. But it all happened too quickly.

And Kacey... It was never my plan for her to get hurt, same as Flynn, as mentioned earlier. But I always knew she'd be in danger. A shame they're the ones who got caught in the storm.

You'll excuse my handwriting; I'm writing this quickly in between moving corpses. It's hard to be alone for extended periods of time at the moment, they're all watching carefully. I write passages anytime I have a moment where it makes sense for me to be temporarily alone.

Melissa... Oh, Melissa. I thought you were better than this. I expected it of Charlie,

but now I have no choice but to take action. What has Leon ever done to her to deserve this? With his own sister? My god. I am sick and tired of this family's corruption, it keeps spreading to unsuspecting souls, surprising me at every turn. I have to gouge it out before it festers further.

～

Well, things took an unexpected turn. Charlie's revealed to me some interesting things, about Leon and herself. Since I arrived here I noticed some inconsistencies with Leon and my perception of him. He's proven selfish, sneaky, underhanded, and almost indifferent to the circumstances. And now I learn he acted unfairly towards his sister all those years ago, and his deception has led the family to take his side in everything, leaving Charlie alone and judged unjustly. I played my part in this. I must make amends. Against all expectations, I have taken a liking to Charlie. I only now understand her. I was planning to see her die, but I will endeavour to help her survive. She deserves a new beginning, with all the Morrison rot out of her life.

～

I tried not to kill Norah. If she'd stayed in bed the entire time, she might have made it out. Not that she deserved to get out alive, but I felt her death would have been pointless. She's already coming to the end of her life and she's caused all the pain she could have caused. Seeing her family dwindle to nothing would probably have been fair punishment. But at breakfast this morning, she smelled me. Must have been the mint.

When I'm nervous, I always suck on mints. So when I abducted and brought her food, I sucked on mints. And ever since the first night, when I syphoned the petrol out of the cars, I continually sucked on mints, afraid someone would smell the petrol on me. And at breakfast I saw her pause and look at every one of us. My blood froze and I was terrified. I thought she'd accuse me, recognise me in some way. She didn't, and that was lucky. But it made me realise I couldn't take the risk to let her live. So before we left to explore the surroundings outside, I pulled a nail out of a floorboard on the stairs, placed a slice of bread in the oven and turned it on. I knew otherwise Norah would just stay in bed until we returned, and I needed her to use the stairs. The smoke alarm was likely to force her to inspect what had set it off. If she'd missed the nail, then I would've thought of something else.

But she didn't.

～

THE MOMENT PATRICK found the gun, I thought this might happen. All his bottled resentment and frustration towards his brother could not survive the confession that he murdered his son. Violette's revelation, however, shocked me to the core. It was all an accident? And *Violette* was taking things into her own hands? Didn't think she had it in her. Well, detectives, you're welcome. You can now close the case of Timothy Morrison. Violette Morrison abducted the child from his house's front garden, the child escaped and fell into the river. She couldn't save him in time. If you think that my word is the only evidence, and therefore proves nothing, think again. You underestimate me.

I have recorded Violette's own confession with my phone. Slightly later than I wished, but she still mentions how the boy died on the recording. And if there are any survivors, they will be able to confirm this. I have hidden the phone in the chest of drawers in the second floor's middle bedroom. I took the bottom left drawer out, slid the phone onto the floor, and placed the drawer back.

I AM ABOUT to show Alicia and everyone else *the* letter. I've hidden the bottles of liquor and left only one on the dining table. Anyone who drinks from it will die from the poison. Alicia won't drink any of it as she hates whiskey.

My heart is pounding.

35

POST-SCRIPTUM

The dead body of a 25-year-old man was found under a bush along the track to the Morrisons' ancestral home, only about a mile from the main road, covered in dried leaves in what we can only assume was an attempt to keep himself warm. Hypothermia is suspected to be the cause of death.

THANK YOU

Thank you for reading this book. I take great pleasure in writing, but having people read what I write takes it to another level.

If *Thirteen Graves* kept you turning the pages, I'd be incredibly grateful if you took a moment to leave a quick review on Amazon.

It helps more than you know — and I read every one!

Thanks again for reading.
   Orion

ABOUT THE AUTHOR

Orion Grace holds triple Canadian, French, and British citizenship and lives in Wales with his wife and three children. A former professional tennis player, he has a bachelor's degree in finance and a master's degree in international studies. He previously published a science fantasy novel in French. This is his debut novel in English. Visit his website at oriongracebooks.com and follow him on Twitter @OrionGraceBooks.

Printed in Great Britain
by Amazon